A GIRL
LIKE YOU

John Locke is a *New York Times* bestselling author, and was the first self-published author in history to hit the number 1 spot on Kindle. He is the author of the Donovan Creed and Emmett Love series. He lives in Kentucky.

JOHN LOCKE

***** Worthy of 6 Stars! By TRW
I give 5 stars to all John Locke books, I would give 6 stars to this one if I could. Not only is it a page turning thriller – I read the whole thing on the beach in an afternoon – couldn't put it down.

***** A fun read! By Kathy
This novel is chock-full of surprising plot twists and turns from beginning to end. It grips you from page one. I read this book in one evening. It's a fast, fun read for sure.

***** Bingo! Cool. Read this book and you're hooked on Locke. By Karin
Locke keeps the story moving and in such an effortless way. I'm passing it on to my husband. It's been awhile since I've read something sexy: this fits the bill.

***** So Entertaining I just went and downloaded another one.
By Patti Roberts
I read this book over a period of 2 days on my Kindle and loved it! So I have just downloaded another one. I hereby declare that I am a John Locke fan. Do yourself a favor....

***** Life equals Experimentation.
By Jean I just couldn't put the book down. Must Read!

***** 10 stars. By Ally
A wonderful mystery thriller. I love all of them but I think this is just my favorite.

AMAZON.COM

THE DONOVAN CREED SERIES

A GIRL
LIKE YOU

JOHN LOCKE

HEAD
ZEUS

This edition first published in the UK in 2013 by Head of Zeus Ltd

9 7 5 3 1 2 4 6 8

A CIP catalogue record for this book is available from
the British Library.

ISBN (Paperback): 9781781852408
ISBN (eBook): 9781781852415

Printed and bound by CPI Group (UK) Ltd, Croydon, CR0 4YY

Head of Zeus Ltd
Clerkenwell House
45-47 Clerkenwell Green
London EC1R 0HT

www.headofzeus.com

ACKNOWLEDGMENTS

Special thanks to Ricky Locke, for his enthusiastic support and advice, and for understanding Donovan Creed better than I do. Thanks also to my spirited editor, best-selling author Winslow Eliot, who inspires me; and to my amazing publisher and cover designer, the incredibly talented Claudia Jackson, and her wonderful company, Telemachus Press; and their remarkably capable assistant, Terri Himes.

Seeking a word that goes beyond thanks to recognize my best friend, my son Kross, who diligently searches the internet many times a day to report the current standings of my novels; who lovingly reports every 5-star review as if it were a national news story, and is sweet and loyal enough to be heartbroken when I receive anything less.

Warm, loving thoughts to my mother, Maurine Locke, who always looks beyond the language and subject matter I write about, and sees only my heart.

PROLOGUE

MOST PEOPLE WOULD think getting bit on the balls by a water moccasin while sitting on the toilet in their own home would be the worst thing that could happen that day.

Sam Case knew better.

After hopping around like a Zuni Indian rain dancer and shrieking himself hoarse, Sam called 911. The dispatcher, a young man with a velvety voice named Earl—Please—Calm—Down—Sir—I'm—Only—Trying—To—Help—You, tried to make sense of Sam's call. It wasn't working, but Earl had the good sense to tell Sam to unlock his front door.

Sam did, then passed out.

Hours later in Brightside Hospital, Sam pressed the button on the morphine pump and turned his attention to the detectives standing at his bedside.

"Did you catch the snake?" Sam said.

"Not our job," one of them said.

"You're going to what, leave it there?"

"Don't you have a housekeeper or something?" the other one said.

Sam glanced at the second detective. Maybe it was the angle, or the drugs, or the hospital lighting, but the guy appeared to have no eyebrows. Was that possible? He fixed his gaze on the man's face.

"What happened to your eyebrows?"

"Fuck my eyebrows," he snarled.

Sam frowned. "You can't just walk around with no eyebrows and expect people not to pose the question."

The first detective chuckled.

"You think that's funny?" the second one said.

"Sorry, Gene. But yeah, it's funny."

Sam said, "A job like yours, you must encounter children."

Gene said, "So?"

"Kids are honest. They say what's on their mind. What do you tell them when they recoil in horror and shriek, "Oh, dear God! What happened to your fucking eyebrows?""

Gene's face reddened. "Listen, asshole. We can either be friends or I can use your nuts as a speed bag. Which sounds better to you?"

"One would be as unpleasant as the other," Sam said.

"Relax, both of you," the first detective said.

"Who are you?" Sam said to the less creepy detective. "And why are you here?"

"I'm Gene Brightside," he said, then nodded at the other guy. "My partner, Gene Caruso." Caruso showed Sam his middle finger and mouthed the words "fuck you." What Caruso lacked in eyebrows he made up for with an honest-to-God Frito Bandito mustache. Where Brightside sported a navy suit with a red tie and matching pocket square, Caruso had on a brown T-shirt, black leather jacket, and wore a pair of faded Levi's covered in cat hair.

"Fatty acid supplement," Sam said.

"What?"

"You need to upgrade your cat's diet. A pet's coat is a reflection of what it eats."

"What makes you think I have a cat?"

Sam pointed to Caruso's pants. "You've got half a cat. The

rest of it is on your pants."

Caruso looked down at his legs, then back at Sam and said, "Fuck you, Case!"

"Digestible protein," Sam said. "And a fatty acid supplement. Your pet will thank you. Once that's taken care of, maybe we can work on your wardrobe, Superfly."

"How'd you know it was a water moccasin?" Brightside said.

"What?"

"You're in Louisville, Kentucky."

"So?"

"You don't find many water moccasins in this area."

"No shit," Sam said. Then added, "Shouldn't you be asking me how a snake got in my toilet in the first place?"

"You get a good look at the snake?"

Sam studied Detective Brightside's face. "I take Lunesta," he said.

"Lunesta."

"Yeah, that's right. To help me sleep."

Detective Brightside looked at Caruso, then back at Sam. "What's that got to do with the snake?"

"Lunesta works best in a dark room. When I get up in the middle of the night to piss, I keep the lights off. I sit on the toilet to keep from spraying piss on the floor."

"Fascinating," Caruso said.

"Four o'clock this morning, I get up to take a piss. In the dark. I walk from the bed to the master bath…"

"How far is the bed from the master bath?" Brightside said.

"Eleven steps," Sam said. "Twenty-eight-point-six feet."

The Genes looked at each other. "You believe this guy?" Caruso said.

"He's precise," Brightside said. "I'll give him that."

"You want to hear the story or what?" Sam said.

"Please," Brightside said. "Go on."

"I sit on the toilet, start pissing, and suddenly there's a white-hot pain in my nuts. I try to jump up, but can't."

"Why not?"

"Because of the three-foot snake attached to my ball sack."

"How'd you know it was three feet long?"

"I reached between my legs and pulled the motherfucker out of the toilet. Squeezed him hard enough to make him detach his fangs. When he did, I slammed his body against the wall two, three times. Then I flung him on the floor and turned on the lights. It was a water moccasin."

"You kill him?"

"No. He slithered away." Sam looked at Brightside. "How convenient, right?"

Brightside said, "This hospital was named after my father, Robin Brightside."

"That's a random thing to say."

"I just meant if there's anything you need, I'll personally ask the staff."

Sam said, "If your family's that wealthy, how'd you wind up a detective?"

"The old man died and left all his money to a bimbo. But the staff is sympathetic to me. Again, anything you need, I can help you."

"Thanks. I'll let you know."

Brightside nodded.

Caruso said, "Did it hurt? Getting your nut sack bit by a water moccasin?"

Sam gave him a withering look.

Brightside said, "The police did a walk-through while you

were on the way to the hospital. According to them, all the doors and windows were locked, except the front door."

"I unlocked the front door so the paramedics could get in."

"After the snake bit you?"

Sam said, "Are you really that stupid? Or are you just fucking with me?"

Brightside said, "I was wondering why the alarm didn't go off when you opened the door."

Sam's look made it apparent he hadn't considered that fact. "I must've forgot to set it that night."

"You have any idea who put a snake in your toilet?" Brightside finally asked.

Sam knew exactly who put it there.

And why.

But what he said was, "I have no idea."

1.

24 Hours Earlier...

THE NYAC IS widely considered the world's greatest athletic club. Located at 180 Central Park South, the 21-story structure boasts 300 guest rooms, a boxing ring, swimming pool, billiards room that overlooks the park, two handball courts, and a number of meeting rooms. The exterior is limestone and concrete, crafted with an Italian Renaissance influence.

When I'm in the city, that's where I go to work out. You want to find me, come early. Ask for Donovan Creed.

Today I'm miles away from the NYAC. I'm across town, in the financial district, standing in front of the New York Gentlemen's Gym. The NYGG is twice as plush as the NYAC, if you can just imagine. I'm wearing olive cargo pants and a Dri-Fit training tee, carrying the vintage leather gym bag that had been used on at least one occasion by the Manassa Mauler himself, Jack Dempsey.

Upon entering, the first thing I see is two security guys in the lobby, talking. I stand a few feet away from them and wait politely till they're finished. Short, wide guy with a hand-stitched tapered shirt is younger, with a no-nonsense air of aggression. He looks me over, sizing me up.

"Need somethin'?" He says.

"Billy King here yet?"

He looks me up and down a second time, then looks at his friend.

Short, wide guy juts his chin toward the double doors.

"Boxing ring's in there," he says. "Billy's in it, poundin' turds outta some poor sap."

I nod.

There's a check-in area, but no one's manning the station.

Second security guy is older, maybe fifty. He's average height, lanky, weighs half as much as his muscle-bound friend. His eyes are kindly, and blue, and framed by ancient scar tissue. In a fair fight between them, my money's on the older guy.

He looks at my gym bag.

"That's a hell of a nice bag," he says. "A classic."

The three of us stand there, looking at my classic gym bag.

Older guy says, "Mind if I have a look inside?"

"What's your name?" I say.

"Does it matter?"

"The police might want a statement later on. I don't want to have to refer to you as 'young guy' and 'older guy'."

"That's funny," older guy says.

"Why's that?"

"My name's Guy," he says.

"No shit?"

"Swear to God."

"Now there's a coincidence."

"And you are?"

"Donovan Creed."

I look at the young guy. He says, "What?"

"Your name," Guy says.

"Why does he care?" younger guard says.

"I might need a witness later," I say.

8

He shrugs. He's so muscle-bound, the simple effort of lifting his shoulders nearly doubles the volume of his neck.

"You can call me Z."

"Z," I say.

"That's right."

"That your street name?"

"You got a problem with that?"

Z and I are looking at each other, but out of the corner of my eye I see Guy roll his eyes the slightest bit.

"Guy, Z, nice to meet you," I say, turning toward the door that leads to the boxing ring.

"Mr. Creed?" Guy says.

I turn my head.

"Your gym bag?" he says.

"Oh, right."

I hand it to him. The bag is an ancient leather boxing duffel, circa 1919, with a single compartment, accessed by a zipper that runs the full length on top of the bag. Guy unzips it, looks inside.

Z says, "What's he got, usual assortment of guns, knives and bombs?" He laughs.

Guy holds the bag open so Z can see the contents.

Z frowns and shakes his head. "Dude. If you're here to fight Billy 'the Kid' King, you oughta turn around and haul ass before he sees you."

"Why's that?"

"He's a three-time former Golden Gloves champion. And he's half your age."

I nod.

Z looks exasperated. "And he's never been beat."

"So far," I say.

Z turns to his friend and says, "You believe this guy?"

Guy says, "What'd he do, push you in the street? Embarrass you in front of your girlfriend? Then challenge you to a fight?"

"He made an unsavory remark about my therapist."

Z says, "Your *therapist*?"

I nod.

"What, are you *nuts* or somethin'?"

"Somethin'."

"And you mouthed off to him?"

"Nope. My therapist did. Then she slapped him."

"So what happened?"

"He broke her nose."

Guy says, "Sounds like Billy."

Z says, "You *saw* it? You were *there*?"

I smile and say, "Had I been there, Billy wouldn't be *here*. He'd be in the hospital, or dead."

Z laughs. "You're big, I'll give you that. And you look tough, and *talk* tough."

"And he's got confidence," Guy adds.

"He's got that in spades," Z agrees. "But Billy ain't never been beat. And like I say, he's half your age."

I nod. "Thanks, guys."

Guy says, "Wait. He's got this move." Then he demonstrates a left hook to the body, followed by a left hook to the chin.

"Thanks," I say. "I'll look for it."

2.

I GO THROUGH the door, see the boxing ring, and sure enough, there's a guy in it beating some poor shlub half to death. You can see the other guy wants to quit, but his pride is keeping him in it. Billy King is taunting him.

"I'd love to see it go the other way just once," a voice says, to my left.

I turn and see a frail young man of about thirty in a wheelchair. He looks vaguely familiar, but I can't place him.

I nod.

"How you doing?" I say.

He smiles. "I'm all right. You here to fight Billy?"

"If he's into it."

He laughs. "Oh, he'll be into it, all right."

He reaches his hand up to shake mine. He's about ten feet away, which means I'd have to walk over to him to take it.

"I don't shake hands with strangers," I say. "Nothing personal."

"Oh," he says. Then says, "What, you got a germ thing?" He pauses. "Or maybe you don't like gimps."

I don't shake hands with strangers because it's an easy way to get pulled into a knife they might have in their other hand, or the knee they might try to slam into my face. Or they might be able to pull me off balance, or hold me while their friends attack me from the back. There are a million reasons I don't shake hands with strangers.

Only one of them is the germ thing.

So he got that one right. But he's sort of right about the other as well, because I especially don't shake hands with wheelchair-bound strangers. One of the deadliest men I've ever met is a wheelchair-bound midget named Victor. As I've learned over the years, a wheelchair can be wired with explosives and conceal any number of weapons. The guy could have a spray bottle filled with cyanide under the blanket that's covering his legs. The guy could have a grenade launcher built into the arm rest. The guy could...well, you get the picture.

I tell the wheelchair guy, "I said it was nothing personal."

"So you did," he says.

Then he does something that completely surprises me. He gets to his feet and takes a few shaky steps toward me.

"Holy Jesus!" he says. "I can *walk*! It's a *miracle*!" Then he makes a whispering sound like "Waaaauuu!" as if there are thousands of people applauding all around us. He stops, straightens up, does a quick little shadow dance that looks all knees and elbows.

"Jimmy Christmas," he says, extending his hand. "Former Lightweight Champion, South Bronx Golden Gloves."

I doubt this kid was the boxing champion of anything. I look at him and think he couldn't beat up my breakfast. But why antagonize him? He seems a decent sort.

"Christmas?" I ignore the hand he's holding between us, waiting for me to shake.

He flashes a toothy grin. "You love it, right?"

"Why Christmas?"

"Because," he says, with a gleam in his eye, pausing to create a build-up. "Like Santa...I deliver the goods!"

He does that whispering "Waaaauuu!" sound again, like he's in an arena and the crowd is cheering wildly.

"Why not call yourself Jimmy Santa?"

A hard look crosses his face. "You makin' fun of my boxing name?"

"Not at all."

"Sounds like you were."

"If I were making fun of your name I'd tell you to call yourself Jimmy UPS."

That throws him a second. Then he says, "Because UPS delivers?"

"That's right. And because they're into boxing in a big way."

He frowns. "But you didn't say that. About me being UPS."

"No, I didn't."

"But you could have."

Was he serious?

"Right. I could have said that. But didn't."

His eyes study my face a few seconds. Then he grins his toothy grin and says, "Tell you the truth, I like Jimmy Santa. You care if I use it?"

"Knock yourself out, Jimmy."

He gives me another funny look. His hand is still hanging out there between us. I can't imagine what sort of clue this kid needs before he understands I'm not going to shake his hand.

"What's with the wheelchair?" I say.

Jimmy Santa shrugs, looks to either side, as if making sure no one's listening. "I'm sorta runnin' an insurance scam while I'm between fights."

I think if he's lucky he'll be between fights a long time.

He says, "My brother's Philip Ward."

I finally make the connection.

"I saw you working Phil's corner last year in Vegas," I say. "Helluva fighter, your brother."

He nods.

The room we're in is set up like an auditorium, with four tiers that can accommodate about 200 chairs for a boxing event. Each tier is stepped down about twelve inches, which means we're standing about five feet higher than the dozen or so guys at ringside, who watch as Billy circles his fallen prey. He's shouting "Get up!" to a guy who can't hear him. Most of the guys around the ring look sick to their stomachs. Probably friends of the poor bastard that's had his ass handed to him.

"Billy's good," he says.

"Damn good," I say.

"Could've been Cruiserweight Champion of the World, maybe," Jimmy Santa says.

"Why isn't he?"

"His father died and left him a successful company. Brokerage firm, he calls it. You know what that is?"

"I do."

We watch the corner guys elevate Billy's opponent. Jimmy says, "Tall one on the left?"

"Yeah?"

"Medical student."

"He's going to have his work cut out for him."

Billy King's walking back and forth on the far side of the ring like a caged tiger. He's not just warmed up, he's juiced. Steroids, probably. Or coke. He shouts, "Who's next? Anyone else?"

"That your cue?" Jimmy says.

"It is." I raise my hand and shout "Next!"

Jimmy says, "I s'pect my brother could handle Billy."

"I s'pect you're right."

14

"Not many others could."

"I'll handle him," I say.

Jimmy smiled. "You look a bit long in the tooth, you don't mind my sayin'."

I smile. "Nice to meet you."

I turn and walk toward the ring a few steps, then stop and turn back to him. Jimmy's hand is still extended. I walk back to him and take it.

"Donovan Creed," I say.

Jimmy smiles broadly. "Jimmy Santa," he says.

"Former Lightweight Champion, South Bronx Golden Gloves," I say.

"Waaaauuu!" he whisper-shouts.

I start heading toward the ring to meet Billy "the Kid" King up close and personal.

"Wait a minute," Jimmy says.

I turn my head.

"He's got this move," Jimmy says, demonstrating a right cross that flies halfway toward an imaginary target, then hesitates, before snapping forward.

"Check hook," I say.

Jimmy gives me a 'thumbs-up.' Then he says, "You want me to work your corner?"

I shake my head.

"Why not?" he says.

"It's not going to last that long."

3.

I STEP DOWN the levels until I'm at ringside. Billy sees me standing there with my gym bag. He trots over, spits on the canvas, and rubs his crotch.

Apparently Billy King has a lot of moves.

"Who the fuck're you?" he says, leaning over the ropes, leering down at me.

"Donovan Creed."

"Donovan? *Donovan?*" He looks around for approval. "What're you, gay?"

"Compensatory displacement."

"What?"

I looked at my watch. "I hate to rush you, but can we move this along? I've got someplace to be."

His nostrils flared, and his eyes were wild. He was definitely on something. Crack, maybe, or PCP. But if PCP, he was simply fortified with it, not completely whacked. I saw a six-foot-five, three-hundred-pound guy in a bar once in New Orleans who was so high on PCP, when a cop came in to arrest him, he broke a bottle and used it to gouge his own eye out. Then he started laughing and stripped off all his clothes, jumped onto a table top and defecated. It took the cop a full minute to realize what he'd just witnessed. He looked at the bloody eye socket, the steaming pile of shit, then turned and ran out the door, gagging. He practically vomited his spleen

16

out in the parking lot. By the time he finished puking, all the other bar folk, including the bartender, were vomiting alongside him. Which made it just two people inside the bar: me, and the naked, one-eyed, three-hundred-pound table shitter.

I had a helluva time kicking that guy's ass.

Billy, though highly skilled, would be a walk in the park compared to him.

"If you've got gloves in that bag, put 'em on," Billy King says. "'Cos I'm not just gonna whip your ass, I'm gonna make you my bitch."

"Compensatory displacement," I say.

"Stop saying that. What are you, retarded?"

"You can wear gloves if you think you need them," I say, "to protect your hands. Of course, I don't plan to hit your hands."

"You can't fight in the ring without gloves," he says.

"Why not?"

"What do you mean, 'why not?' They got rules," he sputtered.

"Then climb out of the ring and fight me here."

He glanced at the activity in the opposite corner. The med student was checking over the guy on the stool. Billy King turned his attention back to me and stared at me as if he were inspecting a bug he'd crushed under his shoe.

"What's in the bag?" he says.

I hold it open so he can see the pen and single sheet of paper. I remove them and hold the paper up to him.

"The fuck is that?" he says.

I notice Guy and Z have entered the room and are standing by the doors.

"Don't mind us," Guy calls out. "We just want to watch."

I nod.

"What's it say on the paper?" Billy repeats.

"It's a release. And down here on the left is where we'll get the witnesses to sign."

"A release for what?"

"In case I kill you by mistake."

"*You*? Kill *me*?"

"Yeah, that's right."

"I could shit you for breakfast!" he says.

I wait.

He says, "Are you fuckin' serious? Because I will flat fuck you up! I'll make you my *plaything*! You'll be doin' my laundry, pretty boy, and takin' it in the ass when I come home after a hard day's work."

"So…you gonna sign it or what?" I say.

He yells at the men in the opposite corner. "Get that bitch outta my ring, and get this old motherfucker—"

He looks at me and says, "What are you, forty?"

"I'd rather not say. I'm sensitive about my age."

"Get this old motherfucker a pair of gloves."

4.

THERE ARE A number of rules for winning a fist fight. Chief among them is, don't fight your opponent the way he wants to fight you. I put the release back in my bag, hop onto the lip of the ring, slide under the ropes. Then get to my feet and stand directly in front of Billy "the Kid" King.

"I'm not fighting you without gloves," he says.

"It's quicker to take yours off than wrap my hands."

"You might get in a lucky punch. It's not fair."

"*You* might get in a lucky punch. I'm willing to take the risk."

"You tryin' to make me look bad? In my own gym?" he shouts, and launches his lightning-fast left jab.

I may be twice his age, but I'm light years faster. I can see it's a feint. I can tell it's going to stop an inch from my right eye. He's throwing it to make me flinch. But I don't flinch. I don't even blink. Instead, I say, "Compensatory displacement is when you substitute something for the thing you don't have."

"What?"

"The thing that makes you feel inferior."

"Oh yeah? And what's that, smart guy?"

"You lack courage. So you overcompensate by calling me names you think will emasculate me."

"I'll show you courage!" he says, and throws a left hook

with bad intentions. I lift my right arm and catch his gloved fist in my hand, the same way Jack Johnson used to taunt his opponents. Then, in one quick motion, I release his glove, slap his face, then grab his glove again. He tries to pull it away, but I don't allow it. Then I release his glove again, and slap his face again. The guys in the corner start snickering.

Billy isn't snickering. He doesn't like what's happening. Doesn't like it at all. When he shifts his feet I see his plan. He's going to shove me, get me off balance, then finish me with an overhand right. But I sidestep him, grab his arm, and use his momentum to hurl him into the ropes. He bounces off and comes at me, forgetting his jab. Throws a roundhouse right, but can't find me because...

Because I'm on my back, on the floor, snaking my legs between his ankles so fast he doesn't have time to regain his balance. I spin my body, and Billy "the Kid" King hits the canvas, face first. I jump to my feet and wait for him to do the same, but he lays there, stone cold. I turn him over and tell the guys who were working the corner earlier to elevate him so he doesn't choke on the blood from his broken nose.

I slide under the ropes, hop out of the ring. Jimmy, grinning ear to ear, meets me there and says, "...And *new* Cruiserweight Champion of the World!" Then does that "Waaaauuu!" thing again.

I open my bag, pull out the picture I took of Miranda Rodriguez yesterday, when I saw her bandaged face. I skitter the picture across the canvas to where the guys are working on Billy King.

"When he comes to," I say, "show him the picture and tell him to stay away from her." I stare at them until one of the guys nods.

I say, "Tell Billy I come to New York City four times a year."

The guy nods again, says, "Okay."

I say, "Then tell him every time I come here, for the rest of my life, I'm going to find him and break his nose again."

"Jesus!" the guy says.

5.

WHEN I ENTER the room, Miranda Rodriguez looks at her watch.

"You're late, Mr. Creed. Punctuality says a lot about a person."

"I'm sorry. I had some business across town."

I take the chair opposite her and notice she's studying me. I say, "I hope you don't mind my dressing casual today. I tried to squeeze in a workout, and hadn't anticipated the traffic."

"Manhattan traffic is legendary. As often as you come to the city, I should think you'd know what to expect."

I put my hands up. "Guilty. Sorry to keep you waiting." I look at my watch and frown. "Not to be critical," I say, "but I'm only two minutes late."

She smiles wistfully and says, "Some people live a lifetime in two minutes."

"Oh yeah? Name one."

She says, "Are we contentious today?"

"Possibly. How's your nose?"

"Broken. But better, thanks for asking."

"And you still won't tell me who hit you?"

"No."

"Why?"

She sighs. "You have a classic hero complex. I have no doubt but what you'd run off and try to hurt the man, and possibly get yourself hurt in the process. Neither of those events would please me, and neither would change what happened."

"It might prevent him from doing it to someone else."

"I've filed an assault report. I'm sure the police will track him down and take him in for questioning."

"And what if he comes after you because you filed the police report?"

"I'll cross that bridge when I come to it."

"I could prevent all that," I say.

"Thank you, Donovan. Truly. I know you mean well, but your tendency toward violence is something I don't approve of. Speaking of which, have you thought about what I said yesterday about compensatory displacement?"

"I have. I even managed to use it in a sentence this morning."

"Excellent," Miranda says. She pauses. "What would you like to talk about today?"

"Tell me about this hero complex disorder."

She nods. "Well, let me start by saying it's not a disorder. Not officially."

"But you think it should be."

"I do. In extreme cases."

"Let me guess: you consider me an extreme case."

"I do. Nothing personal."

"Can you explain it to me?"

"I can try," she says. "The person with a hero complex has a compulsion to save people. Or rescue, or protect them."

"That doesn't sound so bad."

"In extreme cases, he or she actually believes they're making the world safe from some type of perceived threat that only they can prevent."

"I still fail to see the problem. Seems if there were more of us, the world would be a safer place."

She smiles. "Please note my use of the word 'compulsion'. It's one thing to help others because you want to."

"I want to."

"Do you, Donovan? Or do you feel *compelled* to help them?"

"What's the difference? If people need to be helped, or rescued, *someone's* got to do it."

"Do they?"

"Well, don't they?"

"No, they don't."

"What, you're just going to let some child get abused? Some guy get mugged? Some woman get raped? Some terrorist blow up a building?"

Miranda arches an eyebrow.

That last one just slipped out. Miranda doesn't know that for twelve years I was the CIA's deadliest assassin. Nor is she aware that after leaving the CIA I devoted several years to hunting down and killing suspected terrorists for a clandestine branch of Homeland Security.

"Terrorists?" she says. "That's quite a jump. You began speaking of saving a family unit, man, woman or child. Suddenly you're talking about saving the nation. What's next, the world?"

How did I justify all that killing? I honestly believed I was keeping the world safe.

And still believe it.

So maybe she's onto something. Maybe I am an extreme case.

Miranda's brilliant. Hard to believe she's not a licensed psychotherapist. She certainly will be, some day when she's older. She's working toward her master's degree in Counseling Psychology at NYU. She's been studying psychoanalysis and psychotherapy for years. She's observing me now. Sees I've grown pensive. She frowns.

"I'm sorry, Donovan. I think I may have gone too far."

"No, you were great. Sometimes I forget how good you are at this."

"Thanks. But these sessions are really about you."

I nod.

"Are we terminating the counseling session, then?" she asks.

"We are."

Miranda smiles. "So I can remove these glasses?"

"Yes. Along with the rest of your clothes."

Miranda is not a full-fledged hooker. She's a brilliant student trying to get through college without having to take out a school loan. Her client base is limited to the wealthiest of the wealthy, and to my ultimate sorrow, she has no intention of hooking after she gets her degree. I already miss her. Because in addition to my hero complex, I have abandonment issues.

When I'm in town, Miranda gets a hotel room like the one we're in today. The first time I met her she told me about her course of study, and I thought it would be fun to role-play.

Turns out she was damn good at it.

Too good, in fact.

I have to be careful so she won't figure out how screwed up I really am. I mean, I've got more issues than Kleenex has tissues.

A couple weeks ago Miranda added a client. She took a chance on a wealthy young man with anger issues who owns a successful brokerage firm across town. He called her filthy names and broke her nose.

Miranda quickly removes her clothes and stands before me in her bra and panties. She knows I'm a Time Saver, a person who likes to commit special moments to memory. A skilled Time Saver can freeze all the components of an event—the date, mood, time, temperature, lighting, sights, sounds, scents—everything. Then we store this information in a box in our brains and relive it whenever we wish. It's like opening a time capsule years after an event and having all the wonderful memories spill out.

Miranda knows this about me, and waits while I take it all in. After a moment, I nod.

She removes her bra and waits.

I nod.

She removes her panties and waits.

And waits.

Eventually I motion her to turn around.

She does.

After a few seconds she looks back at me over her shoulder.

I nod.

She turns to face me.

"Want me to take your clothes off?" she says.

"No, I'm good."

I kick off my gym shoes, pull off my socks, then stand to remove my clothes. I take her hand and hold it. I lift it to about a foot from my face, and turn it over, palm side up. I stroke the back of her fingers before kissing her hand. Then I lean close to her, capturing her scent. Her hair is cropped just below the ear. I brush against it with my cheek.

"Did you break his nose for me?" she says.

"I did."

After Billy King punched her, Miranda couldn't go to the police and file an assault report because she'd been soliciting at the time of the incident. So she did the next best thing: waited for me to come to town.

"Was he humiliated?" she says.

"That wasn't my intent."

"I know," she says. "But was he?"

"I think so."

"Thanks, Donovan."

We embrace, then kiss.

She starts leading me to the bedroom, then stops, turns to me and says, "Is he afraid?"

"He was unconscious when I left. But yeah, he's going to live in fear awhile."

She smiles. "Good boy, Donovan. Good, good boy. You've made me very happy. Would you like a doggy treat?"

Miranda has some issues of her own.

6.

IT'S NOON AND I'm in my own hotel room, pouring a sensible amount of single-barrel bourbon into the bar glass I've thoroughly cleaned for the occasion. Some people prefer the uniform flavor of "small batch" bourbon. I'm on board if it's Pappy Van Winkle's 20-year-old family reserve. Otherwise, I'm a single-barrel guy.

I hold the glass up and watch the amber liquid through the light as it dances in the glass.

Those who hate bourbon were likely assaulted at some point in their lives by Standard Bourbon, which is rough, and harsh, and made by dumping the contents of all the warehouse barrels together. Judging bourbon by such criteria is like comparing Justin Bieber to Elvis.

I take a sip and let it play in my mouth while I savor the sweet caramel flavor.

Bourbon takes on the distinctive taste of not just the charred, white-oak barrel it ages in, but also the location in the warehouse where the barrel is stored. The best barrels age in the heart of the warehouse, to be lovingly influenced by Kentucky's variable seasons. "Small batch" is made by blending the finest barrels. "Single barrel" is made by bottling the prime barrels individually. Each is unique, but all are excellent.

I swallow my bourbon and feel the warm kick as it hits the

back of my throat. I take another sip, and think about Miranda.

Miranda may be a student in the classroom, but she's a teacher in the bedroom. I offered to immerse myself in her subject matter for the remainder of the day, but she had an afternoon class. We ordered a couple of sandwiches from room service and ate an early lunch. Then I headed back to my hotel, fired up my computer, checked my investments, and ordered tickets for the eight p.m. showing of *Jersey Boys* at the August Wilson on West 52nd.

Miranda lives in Brooklyn but has never seen the show. Always wanted to, she says, but never got around to it. Most nights she's studying, or entertaining wealthy married clients who can't afford to be seen in public. She has a couple of clients who are single, but they prefer her physical skills to her conversational abilities.

Not me. I love taking her out. I'm thinking pre-theatre dinner at Del Frisco's. After the show, we'll go somewhere fancy and spend an outrageous sum on a couple of terrible drinks, and finish the evening at her place, if it pleases her to be romantic.

I look up the restaurant's phone number on my laptop. As I'm reaching for my cell phone, it rings.

Few people have my number. Nadine Crouch, my former psychiatrist, is one of them. Nadine looks after the mental health of my long-time girlfriend, Rachel Case. If Nadine's calling, it can only mean one thing: Rachel's having an episode. I answer the phone.

"How bad is it this time, Nadine?"

"*Donovan! Thank God!*"

She seems to be hyperventilating.

"Take a deep breath," I say. "It can't be that bad."

It isn't.

It's worse.

She pauses a moment, then says, "Rachel's been kidnapped!"

"What?"

My heart drops into free fall.

Nadine struggles to form the words. "A group of armed men burst into the apartment around four in the morning. They grabbed Rachel, injected something into her, and carried her off."

"Who?"

"They carried her right out the back door!"

"Did they say anything?"

"No words were spoken that I could hear."

"Did you try to stop them?"

"I was in my room, she was in hers. They attacked us at the same time."

"How did you get away?"

"I didn't. They injected something into me."

I look at my watch. "This happened twelve hours ago? Jesus, Nadine, they could be anywhere in the world by now."

She says something I don't hear. I ask her to repeat it.

"Not twelve hours ago, Donovan."

"What do you mean?" I look at my watch again. "Louisville's on Eastern time, right?"

"Yes." There's a short pause, and then she says, "But the attack was three days ago."

I close my eyes, stunned. My stomach feels like it's been gripped by an iron fist. Something's burning my throat, trying to get out. Something made out of ice and bile. I swallow it back down, and wince. This is what I fear most in all the world, that one of my enemies would locate my loved ones and use them to force me to do something I don't want to do.

And that's best-case scenario.

Worst case is they want nothing from me, except revenge.

"Why the hell didn't you call me sooner?"

"Nothing would have pleased me more, believe me," she said, icily. "But I've been dead, off and on, for the past three days."

"Where are you now?"

"Medford. Third floor."

"I'm on my way."

7.

ONE OF THE perks of being incredibly wealthy is the ability to have private jet service available anywhere in the world on a moment's notice. By the time my limo drops me off at Teterboro, the Lear 60 is fueled and the pilots are ready to go.

Minutes later we're at altitude, but I've still got an hour thirty to kill before I can start the search for Rachel. When we land, I'll hit the ground running. I'll thoroughly examine her apartment, then interrogate Nadine until she can remember some tiny detail that can help me figure out what I'm up against.

I look around the jet's interior, restless. I'm worried about Rachel. Can't shake the sick, helpless feeling that's chewing my heart. She needs me, and I can't do anything about it. Not yet, at least. Wherever she is, she's suffering. I can feel it. Maybe the suffering is physical, maybe emotional, I don't know. They could be doing terrible things to her. They could...I need to...I need a diversion. I decide to do what I always do when I can't get Rachel off my mind.

I call another woman.

Of course Miranda's voicemail comes on. She's still in class. I hate to cancel our plans via voice message. For one thing, it's classless. For another, I'm a voicemail toad. I never know how to end the damn things, so I stumble on until I hate myself for sounding so lame. Then I hang up in mid-sentence.

As her "Leave your name and number" message runs out, I hear the beep that tells me it's my turn to speak. So I do. I cancel our plans with an idiotic voice message that tells her we can't have dinner tonight because something came up, but then I remember I have to mention we can't go to the show, either. So I tell her that. Then I remember I hadn't told her about dinner until just now, so I have to tell her dinner was supposed to be a surprise, but I hadn't actually made the reservations because...I hang up, pull the phone away from my ear and frown at it, unable to believe how stupid I sound.

My thoughts turn to Rachel, the love of my life.

You might wonder how I can be madly in love with Rachel while carrying on with women such as Miranda.

Simple.

Rachel and I are taking a break in our relationship. What happened is, she went crazy, and I'm waiting for her to get better. I'd be with her, except that her doctors claim I'm a terrible influence. They say if I *really* care about her, I should stay out of her life. I *do* care, so I stay away for weeks, even months at a time. I mean, I have no intention of walking away forever, of course. Rachel wouldn't want that.

Maybe it's not so simple.

What does appear simple is how the psychiatrists always put it on me. What are they basing it on, the fact that after dating me she went nuts? Big deal. Sure, Rachel's symptoms got worse after we became a couple. But that could've been a timing issue. Maybe she was already going crazy. Or maybe some other variable caused the sudden change in her mental health. I mean, Rachel never ate crawfish until I fried her up a batch on our third date. But you don't hear anyone blaming the crawfish, do you?

I notice the lighted display on the cabin wall. The one that shows we're still an hour from Louisville. I think about fetching a mini bottle of bourbon from the liquor cabinet, but decide to keep my faculties sharp.

I stare at my cell phone some more, then dial another number.

Billy "the Kid" King answers.

"Hi Billy, it's me, Donovan Creed."

He pauses.

I say, "Remember me?"

"Yeah, I remember you. You're the asshole who sucker-kicked me. You broke my nose, you son of a bitch. I hope you're happy."

"Happiness is a state of mind, Billy."

"What's that supposed to mean?"

"Means you bring your own weather to the picnic."

"You're a nutjob. What do you want?"

"I'm planning my schedule for the next few weeks."

"So?"

"How does next Friday look for you?"

"What're you *talking* about?"

"I'm terribly busy, so I can't make any promises at this time. But I'll pencil you in for next Friday, eight a.m. You want to meet at the gym, or should I swing by your office?"

"For what?"

"So I can break your nose again."

"What? I'm not even *healed* yet!"

"I know," I say. "Bad timing. For you, I mean."

He says, "I'm getting a bodyguard. What do you think about that?"

"I think you should find a really good one."

"Oh, I will, don't worry."

"That's the spirit."

"You may not *sound* scared," Billy says, "but you're scared all right. And you *should* be!"

"Well, if I should be, I'll try my best. But make sure he's got insurance. You'd be surprised how many of these guys don't have adequate coverage."

"The fuck?"

"You don't want to get stuck with his medical bills."

"I'm not worried."

"Maybe you should be."

"Why's that?"

"Think how pissed he'll be when he learns you hired him to protect you from me."

"I checked around already," Billy says. "No one knows you."

"You haven't checked high enough."

"What's that supposed to mean?"

"You're checking fighters, right?"

"Yeah, so what?"

"You need to check assassins."

He pauses again. Then hangs up.

8.

MEDFORD IS THE income-producing private hospital I helped Rachel purchase six months ago. The building is a hundred-year-old historical structure comprised of hand-cut stone, built to last. Ten years ago it was completely renovated into the three-story hospital that operates beneath the enormous penthouse apartment where Rachel Case lives with Nadine Crouch, my former psychiatrist. Nadine has been quietly caring for Rachel for months.

It takes me two hours to check every square inch of Rachel's penthouse. But it's what I find in her bedroom that tells me all I need to know: a single juice box, lying on the floor by the baseboard. The box was clearly hurled at the first person that entered her bedroom, and the pattern it made on the wall, the door, and the floor clearly identified…

Nothing.

I'm kidding about finding a clue.

I mean, there is a juice box on the floor, and a stain from where she'd hurled it, but unless I run into someone with a juice box stain on their clothes, I've got squat. I check the answering machine. No messages. I check the mail pile. Nothing out of the ordinary. I check the back door and see that no marks were made to gain entry. I check the stairs they would have used to enter, and know they had Rachel on this very staircase three days ago. I take the stairs one flight down to visit Nadine.

"How do you feel?" I ask.

"Terrible."

I believe her. She looks terrible. Then again, she suffered a heart attack and was in a coma for several days.

"Have you been to the apartment?" she says.

"I have."

"Find anything?"

"Nope."

She nods.

I say, "How many of them were there?"

"Five, I think."

"You think?"

"I saw five. Two with Rachel, two with me, one in the living room by the back door."

"No one on the front door?"

She closes her eyes, thinking about it.

"I can't say for certain. There was probably another one at that door. I didn't see him."

"All men?"

"Yes. Far as I could tell."

"Did they all wear the same type of clothes?"

"The ones I saw, yes."

"Were their faces covered?"

"Yes."

"Any insignias on their clothing?"

She thinks a minute. "No."

I nod. "Did there seem to be one person in charge?"

"Yes."

"Where was he?"

"In the hallway."

"In the—Wait. So there were at least six people, not five."

"Right."

I shake my head. "Nadine, you're going to have to do better."

"I'm sorry, Donovan. Between the drugs and what I've been through, it's hard to be precise about these sorts of details."

"Okay," I say. "Let's forget about the men who took her. For now. We can revisit this later, if necessary."

"Okay."

"Tell me everyone who's been to the apartment in the past two weeks."

"No one's been there."

"No pizza or Chinese food delivery?"

"No."

"No mailman? No pest control guy?"

She thinks a moment. "No. The mailman delivers to the box in the hall. Pest control is once a month, scheduled for next week."

"Any packages get delivered recently?"

She shakes her head.

"You're certain?"

"Positive."

"Okay. Tell me every place you and Rachel have been the past two weeks."

"Easy. We haven't been anyplace."

"I doubt that. A spa treatment? Hair salon? Nail salon? Walk in the park? A doctor's appointment? A dentist?"

"No. I mean, I walk in the park, but not Rachel. She uses her elliptical machine."

"When you're in the park, does she answer the door?"

"Never."

"And you haven't been shopping?"

"Not the past two weeks."

"Why not?"

"Her behavior's been erratic. I've purposely kept her inside. She was actually improving the night before the kidnapping. I probably would have taken her out that day…"

Her voice trailed off.

"What?"

"There was a doctor's appointment," she says.

"When?"

"Ten or twelve days ago, I can't remember exactly."

"What day of the week?"

"Monday."

"So…Monday before last?"

"Yes, that's right."

"Eleven days. What type of doctor?"

"General Practitioner."

"Was she sick? Did she hurt herself somehow?"

"No. I set it up after she mentioned she hadn't been to the doctor in ten years."

"Ten years? How is that possible?"

"She's got a needle phobia. She's never given blood."

"Never? What about before she got married?"

"She and Sam got married in Vegas."

"So you got her to give blood?"

"I did. But she was very unhappy about it afterward."

"She was mad at you."

"Yes."

"Dangerously so?"

"I…wasn't sure."

"So you kept her sedated?"

She nods. "At night."

That was probably wise. I always sedated Rachel at night to keep her from killing me in my sleep. Don't get me wrong, she's a great girl. But hey, she ain't perfect, you know?

9.

DR. D'ANGELO'S OFFICE is located downtown on the corner of 4th and Spring, in the Davenport Medical Center. But I can't get there before closing time, so I do the next best thing: talk Ruth Henry, Dr. D'Angelo's long-time receptionist, into having a cup of coffee with me.

We're sitting in Mocha Madness Coffee Shop, across the street from the Medical Center, when Ruth says, "You are absolutely the most handsome man I've ever seen in person."

It's true.

I'm amazingly good-looking. I take no pride in it, since this isn't the face I was born with. In fact, it took a team of plastic surgeons three years to create this face, and they only did it to keep my cover from being blown. Would've cost taxpayers a million dollars had I allowed Uncle Sugar to pick up the tab. But that wouldn't have been fair, since I'm the one who put my cover at risk in the first place. Look, it's a long story. Maybe someday I'll write a book about how it all went down. Till then, try to accept the fact that I'm stupidly good-looking.

"I was heartbroken to hear about Dr. Dee," I say. In truth, I was stunned when I called his office earlier and learned he'd recently passed away.

Ruth shows me a weary smile. "Normally I wouldn't have met you, based on your phone call," she says.

"Why's that?"

"For one thing, you called just before closing time, and I'm usually busy on Friday afternoons."

"I got lucky."

"You did."

"What's the other reason you wouldn't have met me?"

"Because, no offense, I don't recall Dr. D'Angelo ever having mentioned your name. But when you called him Dee, I knew you had to be an old college friend, in for the funeral tomorrow."

I nod. The only reason I knew to call him Dee was because he'd been flirting with Rachel during the exam. "Please," he'd said. "Call me Dee." This, according to Nadine. Proving once again it's the smallest bits of information that make the biggest difference in an investigation.

"Had I known what you looked like," Ruth continues, "I would've got myself all gussied up!"

"Well, you look fine to me," I say.

She winks. "A couple of the girls are working late at the office. I'd give anything if they came in and saw us together!"

I give her my best "aw, shucks" smile.

"I love your dimples," she says.

Of course she does. My face was *designed* to make women love my dimples. The dimples *alone* cost a quarter-mill.

"How's your latte?" I say.

"Excellent, thanks."

Ms. Henry is in her mid-forties and gone to seed. Her hairstyle is ten years out of date, and it appears she put her lipstick on with a paint roller. She has the teeth and fingertips of a chain smoker, the ticks and jitters of a caffeine junkie There is some sort of odd growth above her left eye that resembles a button mushroom someone jabbed with a fork. A yellow Livestrong bracelet circles her right wrist.

"Are you an athlete?" I say, shamelessly.

She follows my gaze to the bracelet, fingers it a moment. "This? Oh no," she laughs. "One of the girls at the office was giving them out. I just like the color."

"It's fetching," I say. Then shake my head in sadness.

"What happened to our poor Dee?" I lament.

"Myocardial infarction," she says, sadly. "Commonly known as heart attack."

I nod, as if grateful for the translation. "Did he have a history of heart trouble?"

"He had chest pains a couple years ago. Had it checked out. He carried nitro in his pocket in case it happened again."

"Did it?"

"Not to my knowledge."

"So it was a surprise?"

"A complete and utter shock."

"You're still working."

"I am. In this town there's always another doctor ready to step up to the plate."

She looks out the window. "That your limo?"

"It is."

"Nice."

I waited until she turned her attention back to me. Then said, "How'd you learn about Dee's passing?"

"Oh. Well, when he didn't show up, I called his cell phone and got no answer. So I called his girlfriend, Lilly. She went over there, found him dead."

"Over where, his home?"

"Yes. On Mulber Road."

"And this was on?"

She takes a long sip before answering, "Tuesday."

Her mouth is now rimmed in red lipstick and white foam.

"So he passed on Monday night?" I say.

"According to his kids, early Tuesday morning. Between midnight and six, they think."

I nod solemnly, but inside I'm jumping for joy because these events add up to more than coincidence. Nadine took Rachel to see Dr. Dee for a blood test. Eight days later he and Nadine suffered heart attacks on the same morning that Rachel was kidnapped by a professional extraction team. Why does this make me so happy? It means Rachel wasn't kidnapped because of me, and I can rule out revenge as a motive for her abduction.

Which means wherever Rachel is, she's almost certainly alive.

Though the death and kidnapping are obviously connected, I have no idea why. According to Nadine, Dr. Dee gave Rachel a cursory exam, flirted with her a bit, and ordered some blood work. A few days later, he's dead and she's gone.

But why?

The only conclusion I can make at this point is Dr. Dee couldn't have kidnapped Rachel. Not that he was a suspect in the first place. Jesus, listen to me: a suspect. What am I, a cop?

Ruth and I chat for another fifteen minutes, during which time I buy her two more mocha lattes. She orders the smallest size each time in order to get her card punched more often, which gets her a free latte for every six she drinks. By my count she's on track to get a free one in thirty minutes.

I finally ask, "Did you happen to meet Nadine Crouch?"

"Crouch?"

"Older lady, friend of my mom's. Before Nadine moved to Louisville, I told her to look up Dee and see if he was taking new patients."

She scrunches her face to force the memory, which causes

the growth on her forehead to shift its position. From this angle I can see several delicate hairs sprouting from it. She catches me staring.

"You like my beauty mark?" she says.

"I've never seen anything quite like it," I say, honestly.

She smiles. "When I was younger, I wanted to have it removed."

"No!"

"I did. I used to hate it."

"You're kidding, right?"

"Well, you know how it is. Kids can be cruel. When you're young..." Her words trail off while she thinks about being young.

"Now, of course, I wouldn't trade it for the world," she says.

"Of course not!"

She winks. "You wouldn't believe how much dick I get because of this!"

I nearly bolt my sandwich from earlier in the day. "Well, I'm not surprised," I say, winging it as I go. "If I'm not mistaken, my buddy Dee was quite fond of you."

She smiles, punches my arm. "That Dee," she says. Then laughs heartily.

"What?"

"He used to call it my third nipple!"

I share her laugh until she says, "Wanna touch it?"

What I want to do is cut that abomination off her head and feed it to whoever kidnapped Rachel. But God help me, I *do* touch it, and she giggles.

"How long are you planning to stay in town, Joe?" she says, calling me by the name I gave her on the phone.

I force a smile. "Well, I was planning to leave after the

funeral." I wait till she looks up at me, then I wink. "But now I'm not so sure."

She smiles and twists her hair. Then takes a pen from her purse and carefully writes her phone number on the back of a blank appointment card.

"Call me if you decide to stay. We can go somewhere and hoist a glass to Dee's memory."

"You think Dee would mind?"

"Who gives a shit?" she says, and punches me in the arm again.

We laugh about that, and when the laughter dies down she excuses herself and heads to the bathroom. When she comes out I notice she is still bowling-shoe ugly, but her pantyhose is missing.

Her first words are, "I do remember Ms. Crouch."

"You do?"

"I just called Ricki at the office to check on it."

"And?"

"She brought us Rachel Case. Patient Number 18660."

10.

RUTH HAS NEVER ridden in a limousine, and hopes I'll let her get in and circle the block just once. I oblige her. As we complete the turn, my driver, Pete, pulls up beside the coffee shop.

Ruth leans into me and whispers, "Will you hold the door for me when I get out?

"Be glad to," I say.

She whispers, "Good. I don't want Pete to see my panties."

Pete puts the car in park.

"Pete?" I call out.

"Yes sir?"

"Stay put. I've got this."

He nods. I climb out and circle the car and open Ruth's door with a flourish. As she exits the limo, I realize the only way Pete could've seen her panties is if he'd opened her purse. In the space of three seconds I manage to see more of Ruth Henry's anatomy than Paris Hilton, Lindsay Lohan and Britney Spears have revealed, combined.

"You like that, don't you?" she says.

"Very much so," I lie, thinking my driver Pete to be a lucky man.

After agreeing to meet at the funeral tomorrow, Ruth and I say our goodbyes.

On the way back to Rachel's apartment I call Lou Kelly,

my facilitator, and tell him everything I've learned since getting Nadine's phone call seven hours ago. He listens carefully, asking no questions. When I'm done, I ask him what he thinks.

"We don't have enough information yet," Lou says. "But I agree we should check the blood test. I can get the results and have them interpreted if you want."

"Get at least one set of eyes on them before sending them to me. Then I'll have someone at the hospital review them."

"What hospital?"

"There's a hospital below Rachel's apartment, remember? Someone there can help me."

Lou pauses a moment, and I say, "How long will it take?"

"Give me thirty minutes."

"That sounds too quick."

"Well, you've given me the name of the doctor, the date, and Rachel's patient number. That ought to be enough for our guys."

I described Lou Kelly as a facilitator, but he's worlds beyond that. He's also a computer wizard who employs a group of geeks who can access anything in the world that can be accessed. He'd been my right-hand man for years, both at the CIA and afterward, at Sensory Resources, where we teamed up to kill suspected terrorists. Lou found them, I killed them. Now we're semi-retired, but we still do some work together.

I paid Lou an enormous sum of money recently, for helping me steal billions of dollars from the world's most dangerous criminals. To this day he's the one asset I can't afford to lose. We had a temporary falling-out once, when he tried to murder me, but we've moved past that. Our relationship is symbiotic. He continues to make things happen for me, and I continue not to kill him for his disloyalty.

11.

IT TAKES LOU more than an hour to call me back. When he does, the news is bad.

"There's no record of Rachel Case's blood work."

"Could they have lost it?"

"Doesn't matter. There'd still be a record of submission in one of the databases."

"Maybe Dr. Dee used an out of town lab."

"That's what took so long. I checked them all."

"The whole country?"

"The whole world."

"You're kidding."

"Do I sound like I'm kidding?" he says.

"You're taking this personally."

"I don't like it when things go missing. This isn't some routine kidnapping. This is a government thing."

"Well, we assumed that already. They used a professional extraction team."

"Right. But there are lots of government operatives who could've pulled that off. What I'm saying, this goes all the way up."

"And you're basing that on a missing blood test?"

"You keep forgetting I still work for Sensory Resources."

He's right, I do keep forgetting. "So?"

"So when this sort of thing goes down, I'm the guy who

makes the records disappear."

"What are you saying—that whoever's responsible knows Rachel and I have a personal relationship? And you and I have a business one?"

"That's exactly what I'm saying."

We're silent awhile. Eventually I say, "Let's approach it from the other end. Let's say something turned up in Rachel's blood test that was so terrible, so dangerous, they wanted to abduct her and study it."

"That's ridiculous."

"But let's say it's not. What could possibly come out of her blood test that would cause this type of reaction? I mean, they killed her doctor, for God's sake."

"We don't know that."

"Sure we do."

"No," Lou says, "we don't. Not for certain. If we assume the doctor died of natural causes, and that someone wanted Rachel enough to kidnap her and kill Nadine, the blood test becomes irrelevant."

"Except that the blood test suddenly never existed. And the doctor died from a heart attack within the same time frame Nadine suffered one. And we know hers was induced. Thank God she keeps an emergency beeper at her bedside for Rachel. Otherwise, she wouldn't have made it."

Lou pauses. "If you're clinging to the blood test, I have no answer for you. If Rachel had any type of blood disease, the lab would've contacted the doctor, and he would've gotten her to a hospital."

"What if she's a carrier for something the military could use for chemical warfare?"

"Are you listening to yourself?" Lou says. "I mean, I know you're upset about what's happened to Rachel and Nadine.

But sometimes the simple reason is the way to go."

"Which is?"

"If you assume the doctor's death is a coincidence, you're left with an attempted murder and kidnapping. A single event."

"To what end?"

"My best guess?"

"Shoot."

"We stole billions of dollars from warlords and terrorists."

"So?"

"Maybe they want it back."

I think about this a minute. Then say, "Well, I'm not going to sit around and wait for a ransom note."

"What're you going to do?"

"Call someone who might be able to help me find Rachel."

"Who's that?"

"Sam Case."

Lou laughs out loud, then catches himself. "Sorry, Donovan. Didn't mean to laugh with Rachel being kidnapped and all. But you've got to admit it's hilarious about you and Sam working together. I mean, she's still his wife, right?"

"Technically."

"And legally."

"There's that."

"You see the irony, yes?"

"Should be a simple thing," I say. "We both love her, want what's best for her."

Lou chuckles, softly. "I agree there's not a finer mind on the planet than Sam Case's. He's more logical than a super-computer. Spock, from *Star Trek*, could take lessons."

"Sam is so methodical and orderly, he makes Spock look like Richard Simmons," I say.

"You think he'll help you?" Lou says.

"Not in a million years."

"So what are you going to do?"

"Formulate a plan."

"How can I help you?"

"You can start by getting me a snake."

"A snake," Lou says.

"Yeah. One that bites."

"A snake that bites," Lou repeats.

"A snake that will bite a man in the dark."

"How big?"

"At least three feet."

"What species?"

"One that can handle being in water."

"How about a water moccasin?"

"I don't want to *kill* Sam, I just want to encourage him."

"I'm on it. When do you need this three-foot, night-biting, water snake?"

"Midnight tonight. At the back entrance to Sawyer Park, on Lakeland."

"Any magic to that location?"

"It's a mile from Sam's house."

"Burlap bag okay?"

"Yeah, that'll work. You got someone here locally?"

"I can get someone. But it's going to cost you."

"It always does."

"Anything else you need?"

"You still on premises at Sensory?"

"Of course. And by the way, your office is still vacant. They keep expecting you to come back."

"Fat chance. Is the medical center still running?"

"As always. Full staff, twenty-four seven."

"Good. I'm going to need access."

"I can get your code reinstated."

I think about it, working my plan in my head. "I'm going to need a vehicle, and some people."

"This is turning into a major caper," Lou says.

"You up for it?"

"Lay it on me," he says.

And I do.

12.

MY NEXT CALL is to Sam Case, Rachel's husband.

"Case," he says.

"Hi Sam, it's me."

There's a long pause. "I thought we had a deal."

"We do, but I'm fuzzy on the details. Maybe we should meet and discuss it."

"You promised."

"Sam, have you heard from Rachel lately."

"You trying to be funny?"

"The reason I ask, she's been kidnapped."

I wait for a gasp, or an exclamation of shock or surprise, but he gives up nothing.

"Did you hear me Sam?"

"I think you're probably trying to set me up somehow. I can come up with a thousand hows, but not a single why. But I haven't completed my thoughts on it yet."

"Save your thoughts. It's not a set-up. I need your help to find Rachel."

"Uh huh. Why me?"

"You've got every reason to be skeptical."

"Ya think?"

"Yes. I can see why you might not trust me, but—"

"No," Sam says. "Let's not rush past those reasons I might not trust you."

"We're wasting time," I say.

"Indulge me this recap."

I sigh. "Fine."

Sam says, "You lured me into an affair, kidnapped me, forced me to witness a double homicide, kidnapped me a second time, locked me in a container, and came within an inch of killing me."

"That's ancient history. You can't live your life dwelling on the past."

"It was barely a year ago, you asshole. Anyway, I'm not finished. You stole my wife, destroyed my business, and ruined my reputation. You subjected me to physical assault and mental torture. You put my life in danger."

"You already said that."

"No, I didn't. You put my life in danger twice. The second time, by double-crossing my clients."

"Water under the bridge, Sam. Rachel's in trouble."

"You think I give a rat's ass?"

"I do."

"Well, I don't," he says, and slams the phone down.

I wait for Rachel's phone to ring. If I'm right about him caring, her phone is going to ring any second.

Rachel's phone rings.

It's Nadine. She wants to know what I've learned.

"Nadine, unless you've got something new to add, you're going to have to trust me to handle this. Do you?"

"Trust you to handle it? Yes. Have anything new to add? No."

"Then don't call me again. It's distracting. Concentrate on getting better. When I get Rachel back, you'll be the first person I call."

"Be safe, Donovan."

"Take care of yourself, Nadine."

I call Sam again.

"You blinked first," he said.

"What is it with you? I'm trying to save your wife."

"Oh, fuck you, Creed."

"Why are you so antagonistic, Sam?"

"Shall I repeat my list of grievances?"

"No."

"Then let's be clear."

"Let's."

"You're not trying to save my wife. You're trying to save your girlfriend."

"Okay."

"You're conceding the point?"

I sigh loud enough so he can hear. "Yes, Sam, I concede. Now help me find Rachel."

He hangs up again.

"Shit!" I use my cell phone to call Lou. "You got that snake yet?"

"I'm working on it. You said midnight."

"Midnight still works."

Lou pauses. He can tell I'm agitated. Finally he says, "Was there anything else?"

"Yeah. It can be a water moccasin."

"You know your snakes?"

"Mostly."

"It'll be dark. Won't be easy handling a water moccasin in the dark. Or situating it."

"I'll be fine. I'll be able to tell instantly if your guy brings me a poisonous snake."

"How?"

"Because you're going to have him bring me two syringes

with antivenom."

"Okay. No syringe means it's not poisonous."

I pause. "You're not going to use this as an opportunity to come at me again, are you?"

"No. I've learned my lesson."

"Because Callie and I have a pact."

Callie's my lethal associate. She and I agreed a long time ago that if one of us dies, there are three people the surviving one will kill before learning the cause of death. Lou is the first person on that list.

"I know all about the pact. You and I used to have one."

"I'm trying to trust you, Lou," I say.

"I appreciate that, Donovan. It's more than I deserve."

I agree. But what I say is, "We can still do some great things together."

"You'll get her back, Donovan."

"I know. I just hope there's still enough Rachel left in her to build a future with."

13.

SAM'S HOME.

If ever there was a creature of habit, it's Sam. You could set your clock to his routines. It's after eight-thirty, so he's home.

I have Pete take me to Wal-Mart, where I pick up some heavy-duty gloves, goggles, a glass-cutter and a suction cup. I stow those items in one of the two duffel bags I brought to Louisville this afternoon. When Pete drops me off at the abandoned Chevy dealership on Gordon, I tell him to stay in the general area and wait for my call. Carrying one bag in each hand, I cut across two fields and a golf course, which puts me in Sam's backyard. It's dusk, and I can see him moving around in his kitchen. I work my way to a thicket, near a dried-up creek about fifty yards from the sliding glass door that leads to his deck. From there I cut to the evergreens that shield the back of his swimming pool, and take up a prone position among the trees so I can view his windows through my scope.

Sam's house is large, but wide open from the back. Only his bedroom and office windows have curtains. His bedroom curtains are closed, but his office is clearly visible. Sam never closes his office curtains because they're heavy, lined, and when you close them and try to put them back the way they were, they wrinkle. Sam is a meticulous guy. Hates wrinkles. Irons his underwear, he hates wrinkles so much. And his pillowcases, too. And his sheets. I know all this because I secretly lived in his attic for nearly two years and watched his every move through pinhole cameras while plotting to steal his clients' money.

I'm a former sniper, with two years' experience. I know how to remain still, completely soundless, whether laying in a field or living in someone's attic. Proof of that are the seven deer that casually walk from the opposite stand of trees and stop twenty feet from me to chew the green off some low branches. Realizing this means the area is completely free of people, I punch Sam's number into my cell phone. I have a silent key feature, so it's only after I say, "Sam, don't hang up," that the deer freak out and start running in all directions.

"I'm not going to help you, Creed," he says.

"Fine. But at least let me tell you what I've got."

"You're wasting your breath."

I can tell he's about to hang up. I say, "Rachel gave blood eleven days ago."

He pauses. "Rachel doesn't give blood."

In the house, I see the light come on in his office, see Sam take up a seat by his computer.

"Are you with me?" I say.

"Yeah, go ahead."

Sam stands, suddenly, walks to his windows, and looks out. Then he shuts the curtains.

"Pay attention, Sam," I say. "Because I can't do this without you."

"That's obvious. Because I'm the last guy you'd turn to."

"True. For lots of reasons."

"How did you get her to give blood?"

"I don't know. Nadine talked her into it somehow. Anyway, Nadine took Rachel to a doctor's office, a guy named

D'Angelo."

"Go on."

"One of the nurses drew Rachel's blood, sent it to a lab. A week went by, and D'Angelo died from a sudden heart attack."

"What day?"

"Tuesday morning. Between midnight and six a.m."

Sam places me on speaker phone. I hear keyboard strokes, and assume he's checking internet records to verify Dr. Dee's death. After a minute he says, "Go on."

"At four the same morning, a professional extraction team broke into Rachel's apartment. Nadine was given an injection that induced a heart attack. She only survived because of her proximity to the hospital one floor down."

"She had time to get downstairs?"

"No. She pressed her panic button by the nightstand. Someone from the hospital came and got her."

"Someone from the hospital had a key?"

I hadn't thought to ask Nadine about how they knew to come in the back door. I doubt it's important, but this is a perfect example of why I need Sam.

"I doubt they had a key," I say, "but the back door was left unlocked after the break-in. The hospital guys probably tried the front door, couldn't get an answer, went around to the back. It's just around the corner of the hallway, by the stairwell.

"Did they inject Rachel with something?"

"Nadine doesn't know. But I'm sure they did. Rachel would have pitched a fit, otherwise."

"They wanted to keep her alive," Sam says.

"Apparently. But who took her? And why?"

Sam says, "Who do you suspect?"

"Some branch of the government."

"And you're wondering what could show up in Rachel's

60

blood test that would cause that type of reaction."

"Exactly."

"Do the cops suspect foul play in the doctor's death?"

"No."

"But you think there's a link."

"I know there is."

"And you're certain you've narrowed her disappearance to the blood test."

"Yes."

"Then I can't help you," he says, and hangs up.

I wait a few minutes, then leave my bags by the trees and walk to the side of Sam's house, where the roof hangs low over his bathtub. I pull one of the bricks loose, turn it lengthwise, push the end back into the wall where the side had been, making a ledge for my foot. I step on that brick and pull out another one, three feet higher. Then I stand on that one and repeat the process until I have a brick ladder that takes me up to the roof. I have several ways to access Sam's roof, but this is my favorite. I created this brick ladder years ago. There's another one just like it on the other side of his house, where the roof hangs low over his breakfast room.

I follow the incline of the lower roof to the area that gives me access to the next level. I take that to the eave where the stucco meets the brick, where years ago I created a crawl space that's invisible from the ground. I wedge my body underneath that, and open the door I built that leads to the command center I created in Sam's attic back in the days when I was spying on him and Rachel.

In the beginning, I had two command centers in Sam's attic: the one I wanted him to find, and the one I wanted to keep secret. The secret one is tiny, accessible only from the crawl space, and is restricted to one small eave.

The command center Sam knew about didn't have any cameras. Sam always assumed I did my spying after he and Rachel left for work each morning, at which time I roamed through his house, eating his food, using his bathrooms and shower, extracting files and installing programs on his computer.

I power up my old system and immediately see Sam through the pinhole camera I'd placed in his office. There are dozens of these cameras located throughout his house. My old laptop is still connected to the power source. I start it up, expecting to view the keystroke capture device I attached to Sam's computer that will show me everything Sam is typing on his office computer.

But I'm getting nothing, which tells me he's installed a new computer since my last visit.

My little nook is soundproofed, and I'm above the second floor of Sam's enormous house. He's on the first floor. No way he can hear me if I decide to call him again.

So I do.

14.

"HOW'S IT COMING, Sam?"

"I'm not going to help you, Creed."

"There must be some arrangement we can make."

"Nothing comes to mind."

"Money?"

"I've got money."

It's true. I'd given him a cut from the heist. It was only fitting, since I'd put him through hell and destroyed his business.

"I could always torture you."

"Good luck with that."

Also true. There's a very small percentage of people in the world who don't respond to torture. Sam is one of them. It's not that he feels no pain. It's more like he shuts down when subjected to repeated pain. You can shock Sam with pain, but you have to attack him through his mind. The problem with that is, he's smarter than me.

But I'm more cunning.

"Sam, Rachel means the world to me."

"Do you ever listen to yourself? I'm supposed to care about your feelings? Rachel meant the world to me, too, you bastard. I know what it's like to lose her, remember?" He pauses. "Actually, there *is* something you can do to make me help you."

"Name it."

"Promise when we get her back, you'll walk away."

"Done."

"You'll never contact her, never allow her to contact you."

"Okay."

"You'll remove yourself completely from her life. Forever."

I remain silent a moment, allowing the full weight of his words to sink in.

"I agree to your terms," I say.

"You're a lying sack of shit," Sam says. "Your word means nothing. I'm not going to find her just so she can be with you. Wherever she is, whatever they're doing to her, she's better off."

"You don't believe that."

"Goodbye, Creed. Suffer greatly."

He ends the call.

I know he's working downstairs, know in my gut he's making progress. Sam will have this whole thing figured out in an hour or two. Of that I'm certain. But knowing Sam, he'll be content just knowing what happened to Rachel, and why. Because the world is like a puzzle to Sam, and this is just a challenge. Once the puzzle is solved, he'll move on to the next puzzle that turns up.

This detachment is the reason Rachel stopped loving him long before I entered the picture.

I check my watch and see it's three hours till midnight. I call Pete and tell him I'm done for the night. He knows to add an extra twenty percent to the built-in tip charge. In a few hours when I need a ride, I'll take one of Sam's cars. I call Lou again, to work out all the arrangements for what's going to happen after the snake does its job. If the snake doesn't bite Sam when he sits on the toilet, I'll put it in his bed. If that doesn't work, I'll knock Sam unconscious and push its fangs into his chest. Bottom line, I'm not leaving till Sam gets snakebit.

I look at my watch again, and wonder what Miranda is doing instead of being with me.

I wonder where Rachel is, and hope she's being treated humanely. But I worry she's not, since her abductors killed Dr. Dee and tried to kill Nadine.

I set the alarm on the clock in my command center, the one that wakes me with a flashing light instead of a buzzer.

I lie down.

My stomach growls, and I realize I haven't eaten since this morning, so I turn off the alarm, slip out of my command center, climb down the brick ladder on the side of Sam's house, go back through his yard, across the golf course and fields, past the vacant Chevy dealership, and take a seat at the counter of a nearby Steak 'n Shake.

15.

SAM DIDN'T GO to sleep at his usual time.

Being an extremely orderly guy, Sam sticks to a rigid schedule, unless he's working on something important. When he is, he loses all track of time. I'm hoping this project isn't going to stump him. For a guy like Sam, this should be simple. What could be in Rachel's blood test that would frighten the government so badly, they're willing to kill people to keep it hid? There couldn't be many answers to that question. But when I leave his house, Sam is still at his computer.

On the way to the park, I call Lou and ask him to check with the Sensory Resource doctors, who are among the best in the world.

"I already asked them," Lou says.

"And?"

"They have no idea."

I hang up and call Dr. Howard, Chief of Staff, who works the day shift.

When he answers, I say, "Hi Doc, it's Donovan Creed."

"You know what time it is in Virginia?"

"Yeah. Same as Louisville."

He yawns. "How's the face holding up?"

Doc Howard headed the team of plastic surgeons that made me look handsome.

"You made me look like a sissy."

I hear him chuckle.

"I need to ask you something, Doc."

"Can it wait till morning?"

"If it could, you'd still be asleep."

I hear him moving about, probably adjusting himself to a sitting position.

"Okay, shoot," he says.

"A lady named Rachel gets her first blood test ever. When the results come back, something shows up that is so terrible, so horrifying, the government kills Rachel's doctor, and sends a professional extraction team to kidnap her."

"That sounds like the plot of a terrible book."

"Save your review till after I write it. For now, just tell me if it's possible."

He thinks a moment, then says, "No."

"Are you certain?"

He says, "The lady appears to be healthy?"

"Physically, yes. Mentally, she's a mess."

"Can she walk and talk and move around normally?"

"Yes."

"Well, then, to the best of my knowledge, there is nothing to be found in her blood that would frighten anyone outside of her friends and family. If there were abnormal cells or some type of blood disease that hadn't affected her physical health, her doctor would schedule further tests. If her blood work is completely off the charts, she's either ill, or the sample got contaminated. If contaminated, they'd simply repeat the test. Beyond that, the notion of a doctor or lab sharing a random person's blood work with the government is absurd."

I think about what he's told me, and work it around in my head. I know I'm missing something, but have no idea what it could be.

He says, "Are you doing anything dangerous tonight?"

"No, why?"

"You know I live vicariously through your adventures."

I see a van pull up to the park entrance.

"Go back to bed, Doc," I say. As I hang up I hear him shout, "Hey, you're welcome!"

Two minutes later I meet the snake guy.

"Be careful of Frankie," he says. "Water moccasins can bite through burlap."

"Snake's name is Frankie?"

"That's right. Most water moccasins are docile, except when cornered."

"But not Frankie?"

"No sir. Frankie don't let you corner him. He corners you!"

Walking back to Sam's house, carrying the very dangerous Frankie, I hear nothing, but feel plenty. I'm suddenly on the ground and fairly certain someone has shot me in the head with a high-powered rifle.

16.

I'VE BEEN SHOT before, but never in the head, so I'm not positive how I'm supposed to feel less than a millisecond after the hit.

But I'm pretty sure I'm not supposed to be feeling fine.

My first thought is that Lou might have set me up with the snake man, or one of his buddies who may have been hiding near the drop-off spot. But I didn't hear a gunshot. As quiet as it was, I should have heard a gunshot, had there been one, even if the assassin used a silencer.

I wait a few minutes to make sure no one is hanging around to finish me off, then run my hands over my head, but find no lumps or bruises. I realize it's dark, but blood feels like blood regardless of the light conditions, and I don't feel any. Just to make sure, I get to my feet and walk to a lamp post and look at my hands and still find nothing.

Whatever just happened had been internal. Had I suffered a mini-stroke? I lift my hands over my head, something that's supposed to be hard to do if you've had a stroke. I speak out loud: "Sal Bonadello lives in Cincinnati." I repeat the sentence and listen to see if I'm slurring my words. I don't appear to be. Then again, maybe only others would be able to tell.

But I feel fine. Slight headache, nothing more. Whatever it was, lasted only a fraction of a second, but hurt like hell.

Could I have an aneurism? A brain tumor? These are happy thoughts.

I go back and retrieve Frankie the snake from where I'd dropped him, then he and I head for Sam's house.

17.

WHEN I GET back to Sam's and check the camera screens, I
see he's still in his office, working. So I'm stuck in a tiny
cubicle with a poisonous snake that's trying to get out of a
burlap bag. Each time I set the bag on the plywood floor, it
moves toward my leg. I try hanging it from one of the hooks
at the top of the eave, but that puts the bottom of the bag
within inches of my body. I could put Frankie outside, but it's
cool out, and I don't want to make him docile. I decide to let
him hang where he is, and make a point not to get too close.

Thankfully, I don't have to wait too long. Sam shuts his
computer off at one a.m., and heads to the master bathroom
to get ready for bed. He sets the alarm and takes his sleeping
aid, and I wait for it to do its job.

I wait an hour before wrestling Frankie through the crawl
space. He's highly agitated. The bag is thumping and rolling,
and I have to extend it as far as I can from my body. Finding
my way down the brick ladder in the dark is much harder
than climbing up it had been a couple hours earlier, but I
manage.

I know about Sam's alarm system. Specifically, I know he
has contact alarms on all the doors and windows. He also has
glass-break alarms. But if I can cut the glass without shattering
it, I can climb in through his basement window.

Sam thinks he has tempered glass on his basement windows,

71

and he's partially right. I replaced two of the windows while he and Rachel were on vacation in Cancun the first year I lived with them. I set the snake on the ground by the window, and go to the trees to get my duffels. Once back, I remove the equipment I need to cut the glass. I place the suction cup on the windowpane and don my gloves and goggles.

There's some light, but not enough for this job. I dig through my bag until I find one of several penlight flashlights I brought. I flip it on and hold it in my mouth while getting the glass-cutter out.

Forget what you see in the movies. In real life, no one cuts a circle out of a pane of glass. And even if I could, it wouldn't do me any good, because the point of making an opening is to get your hand in the glass so you can crank the window open. Which would set off Sam's alarm.

Sam has a keyless entry, and had he not set his alarm I could have gone to his garage door and punched in the backup code I entered into his system years ago. I'm sure that would still work to get me inside. But Sam sets his alarm to go off instantly when he's home, and even though I set up a backup code for myself that would probably work, the alarm would still be on long enough to wake him up.

So I'm betting the farm on being able to cut a large enough hole in the glass to climb through. Of course, if I botch the job, I'll just knock Sam unconscious and try to beat him into cooperating. It won't work, but it'll make me feel better.

You have to cut a glass window in a single swipe from one side to the other, or top to bottom, using firm pressure through the entire motion. But glass is unstable, and even when your technique is perfect, it can break.

Fortunately, I'm very good at glass-cutting, and quickly open a space large enough to climb through. After doing so, I reach back out through the window and grab the burlap bag. Then I go in the utility room and retrieve the replacement window I'd hidden behind one of the HVAC units a couple years ago, and place it beneath the open one. Lou's clean-up crew will replace the window, giving me continued access to Sam's house in the future, should I desire it. Next, I go up the stairs to the main floor, open Sam's bedroom door, and make my way into his bathroom. Once there, I lift the toilet lid, untie the sack, and dump Frankie into the toilet. He wants out, but he's disoriented enough that I can shut the lid before he escapes.

Then I have a different problem.

Frankie is so agitated he starts thumping the toilet lid. I sit on the lid twenty minutes until he finally gives up. Then I remember Sam's alarm is still set, so I walk to the end of the hall where the alarm panel is located, and type in my alternate code. As I suspected, it works. Then I go back to Sam's closet and hide until I hear the snake banging the lid again. I go back in the bathroom and sit on the lid another ten minutes to keep it in the toilet bowl. The whole time I'm thinking *this is the last time I'm working with a snake*. When Frankie settles down again, it's back to the closet. Around four a.m. I hear Sam get out of bed and trudge to the toilet. I hear the shriek that tells me he's found Frankie, and the blood-curdling scream that tells me he's been bit. I hear him slamming the snake against the wall, and then the bathroom light comes on and he runs for the phone while screaming my name.

I hear him make the call to 911, hear him open the front door.

When Sam passes out, I administer the antivenom, find his cell phone, remove the battery, and put it in his Sponge Bob pajama pocket. Then I go to his bathroom to hunt down the

73

injured snake. I find him instantly, tucked in against the baseboard, under the sink. I work Frankie back in the sack, very carefully, and place him on the front passenger seat of Sam's car. Then I go around to the back of Sam's house, replace the bricks, put my tools in one of the duffel bags, and carry them to the garage and put them in the back seat. Then I go in the house, get Sam's car keys from the countertop where he keeps them, open the garage door, and start the car up. When I get to the end of the driveway, I put Frankie in the mailbox, which is the cue for Lou's guy to come get him. With any luck, Frankie will live to bite again.

As I exit the neighborhood, I see the ambulance approaching Sam's house. Since it's four in the morning, they're not running the siren, just the flashing lights. I pull over to the side of the road, to let it pass, then I drive myself to the private airport where the Lear 60 is waiting to take me to Virginia.

18.

Present Day...

IT'S SATURDAY MORNING, a little after ten.

Detectives Brightside and Caruso have just left Sam's hospital room. I know, because I'm sitting at my old desk at Sensory Resources, watching on my live camera feed. I'm impressed and a little surprised that Sam didn't tell them anything about me. But that's a good thing, I think. It could mean he's decided to help me. Or it could mean he doesn't trust them. Or it could mean nothing. I watch Sam try to reach his cell phone, which has been placed beyond his reach. Not that it matters, since there's no battery in it.

Since nothing's happening in Sam's hospital room, I call Ruth Henry, and break the news that I won't be able to attend Dr. Dee's funeral. While I've got her on the phone, I say, "By the way, I met Nadine last night after talking to you. The young lady she brought to see Dr. Dee was her granddaughter."

Ruth doesn't seem to know how to respond, so I keep talking. "Anyway, Nadine said they were expecting to hear from the office about her blood test results. Do you recall if they ever came back?"

"Well, I'm just the receptionist," Ruth said. "I set the appointments and greet the patients. I don't really get into the actual workings of the office."

"Of course," I say. "Is there someone Nadine should ask for about the blood test?"

"Ricki would be able to answer her questions. But we're closed till Monday."

"Right. By the way, do you happen to know which lab the office uses for blood work?"

"You're going to a lot of trouble to help an old lady friend of the family," Ruth says. "Why don't you come back to town and help me forget about my ex?"

"I'll do it, first chance I get."

"Just so you know, I'll do anything you want."

"What more could a guy ask for?"

"Corlis."

"Excuse me?"

"We use Corlis Medical Laboratory—CML—for our blood work."

"I'll pass it on to Nadine."

"She won't need to contact them. I'll make sure Ricki gives her a call on Monday."

"That's really sweet of you."

"Come on back, I'll show you the definition of sweet."

"I'm practically calling my travel agent already!"

She blows me a kiss goodbye. I return it, then buzz Lou.

"Corlis Medical Laboratory," I say, when he enters my office.

"What's that?"

"The place Dr. Dee sends his patients' blood work."

"I'm sure we scanned them for a match," he says. "But I'll send someone over there to do an on-site search."

"Thanks."

"How's the patient?" Lou says, looking at one of the two screens on my desk. One shows the side view with Sam in the

76

foreground and the doorway behind him. The other shows Sam from the foot of the bed up, so I can focus on his facial reactions.

"No change," I say.

Lou starts to leave, then stops and says, "It's good to see you, Donovan."

"You too, Lou."

He says, "I've got a riddle for you."

"Go ahead."

"Two men are on opposite sides of the earth. One is walking a tightrope between two buildings, at the 95th floor. The other's getting oral sex from a 95-year-old woman. They're both thinking the same thing. What are they thinking?"

I shrug.

"Don't look down!"

I smile and say, "It's good to be back."

Ten minutes after Lou leaves my office, I see movement on the screen, and notice a doctor has entered Sam's room. I turn up the volume.

19.

"MR. CASE, I'M Dr. Elton Drake. I'm afraid I have some bad news."

"Let me guess," Sam says. "The snake died after biting me?"

Dr. Drake gives a humorless smile. "If only."

"Let's hear it, then."

"I'm afraid we're going to have to amputate your left leg."

"*What?*"

"Not the entire leg. Just to the knee."

"Oh, just to the knee? Well, how fortunate for me!" Sam says, sarcastically. Then adds, "This is ridiculous. This isn't the 1800s."

A nurse joins them, and starts fiddling with Sam's IV.

"You were bitten by a water moccasin," Dr. Drake says.

"Big fucking deal. You're not cutting my leg off. There's antivenom available for water moccasin bite. I've read about it."

"You're referring to CroFab, a serum derived from four species of pit vipers."

Sam raises his head, closes his eyes a moment, then opens them and recites, "CroFab is a combination of venom components from American pit vipers including three types of rattlesnakes and the water moccasin."

"Very impressive," Dr. Drake says.

"There's more," Sam says. "Untreated, a water moccasin bite can cause severe pain and tissue damage that can result in the loss of a limb or even death. Treatment with CroFab, within six hours of a snakebite, is virtually always effective."

"Are you finished?"

"No. Use of CroFab is contraindicated in patients with a known hypersensitivity to papaya, or certain pineapple proteins. I have no issues with those fruits, so I'm within the statistical safe range."

"Truly astounding."

Sam waves his arm. "Whatever. My point is, in this day and age, people don't die from viper bites. Nor do they need their legs cut off."

Dr. Drake says, "Are you familiar with S.S.S.?"

"Is that your poor imitation of a hissing snake?"

"Snakebite Severity Score. It's a scale used to assess the severity of envenomation in a patient."

"So?"

"There are six categories. And yours is off the charts."

"You're saying I could die?"

"There's a treatment algorithm. We've followed it carefully. You're already on the maintenance dosing. You'll live, but the damage to your left leg is too severe."

"Why would the poison collect in my lower leg? The bite was on my nuts."

"It just felt that way," Doctor Drake said.

"What do you mean?"

"The snake bit your inner thigh. If we were just talking about that bite, you'd probably be fine by now."

"What do you mean, '*that* bite?'"

"You reported being bit once. But you were also bitten on the calf of your left leg."

"That's impossible."

"The snake must have found you on the floor after you passed out."

"This is the first I've heard about that!"

"Not true. I personally discussed this with you several hours ago."

Sam stared ahead, blankly.

"I'm sorry, Mr. Case, I know this comes as a terrible blow."

"A terrible blow? Ya think? *I'll* tell you a terrible blow: the one I got from your daughter last night. *That's* a terrible blow!"

"There's no reason to attack me personally."

"It's bullshit!" Sam yells. "I'm not allowing it! I won't sign the consent form!"

"Sam, look at me," Dr. Drake says.

Sam does.

"We're trying to save your life here, son."

Sam raises his head again, and closes his eyes. This is how he accesses information he's read in the past. Sam's a genius. He's one of six people in the world who has Superior Autobiographical Memory, the initials of which are why he calls himself Sam. In addition, he is the only one of three people in the world who possess Mega Savant number skills who isn't mentally disabled. Simply put, he is one of six people in the world who can do one thing, one of three who can do another, and the only one in the world who can do both.

Sam opens his eyes and starts reciting, but his heart isn't in it. He's no longer sure of himself, and his words are coming out in a monotone. "Water moccasin bites do not create anaphylactic reactions in their victims. Moreover, their venom does not contain the neurotoxins common to rattlesnake venom. These bites create severe pain and swelling…"

"In most cases, that's correct," Dr. Drake says. "And I have to admit, your knowledge of water moccasin bites is far superior to mine, which is why I had to read up on the subject this morning. But there's one thing you missed."

"What's that?"

"Water moccasin venom contains proteolytic substances that can cause severe tissue destruction."

"I'm not familiar with the term 'proteolytic'."

"It refers to agents that aid in the breakdown and assimilation of proteins."

Sam ponders this explanation a moment, then says, "Something's happening." He looks at the nurse. "What did you just do?"

She looks at Dr. Drake.

Drake says, "She gave you something to relax."

"I don't *want* to relax!"

The Doc motions the nurse to leave. When she does, Sam says, "You should be able to counteract the tissue destruction with a course of antibiotics. Try that, before you go around sawing off people's legs."

"I'm afraid it's gone beyond that."

"Well, I'm not giving my permission. You take my leg off, I'll sue."

"You've already signed the release form, Mr. Case, and you need this amputation to save your life. As a responsible physician—"

Sam struggles to rise to a sitting position. "I never signed any fucking form that gives you permission to cut off my leg! This is complete and utter bullshit! I want to see the Chief of Staff."

Dr. Drake says, "The consent form you signed upon admittance authorizes us to perform any surgery we deem necessary to save your life."

"Yeah, well, I'm rescinding it here and now. What are you smiling about?"

"I'm sorry. It's just that your word choice—rescinding—comes from the Latin words that mean 'to cut off'."

"Yeah, that's really fucking hilarious. Anyone tell you your bedside manner sucks?"

Sam's words are starting to slur. Whatever the nurse gave him has begun taking effect.

"I apologize," Drake says. "But it doesn't change the fact you require this procedure in order to stop tissue destruction at the knee. We're not just saving your life, we're also saving the upper part of your leg. And I can tell you, it's a heck of a lot easier to fit a prosthetic to your knee than it is to fit an entire leg. It's also less dangerous, and the time it takes to adapt is, by comparison, almost insignificant."

"You almost make it sound appealing."

"You'd be amazed how far the science has come."

"Save your enthusiasm for someone who gives a rat's ass. I'll take my chances. First of all, I don't believe any of this. This is one of Creed's bullshit scams."

"I'm afraid I don't understand."

"Where are you, Creed? Hiding under my bed?"

"Mr. Case, please."

"Are you even a doctor?"

"I can assure you, I've been a surgeon here at Brightside since the hospital was established. I know you're upset, and it's clear I could have done a better job explaining your condition. But your current state of agitation demonstrates your inability to make a rational decision about revoking the release you signed. And since your wife has signed the authorization, I really don't understand your—"

"*What?* My *wife?* Wha—what did you just say?"

"Your wife, Rachel. She signed the authorization form, agreeing to the surgery."

"When?"

"We briefed her about an hour ago."

"She's here?"

"Of course."

"You're joking."

"Mr. Case…"

From my office, I press Lou's intercom and shout, "Come quickly."

Sam says, "If Rachel really *was* here, she'd have come in to see me."

"She wanted to wait until after the surgery."

"Send her in. If Rachel's here, send her in."

Dr. Drake sighs and says, "Very well, Mr. Case. I'll ask her. But if she agrees, it's only for a minute. We need to get you prepped for surgery."

As Dr. Drake leaves Sam's room, Lou hustles into my office.

"What's up?"

I point to the screen.

Sam and I, and Lou, are all straining to see what's about to happen.

"What are we looking at?" Lou says.

"Shhh," I say, pointing at the screen.

"But nothing's happening."

I hold my hand up to silence him, while keeping my eyes riveted to the computer monitor in front of me.

A minute goes by, then another. Then the door to Sam's hospital room opens, and Dr. Elton Drake walks in, followed by Rachel Case.

20.

"HOLY SHIT!" I say.

"Is Sam asleep?" Lou says.

"Look at the other screen and tell me. I can't take my eyes off Rachel."

"He's asleep."

Rachel rushes over to the bed and says, "Sam! Wake up!"

She pushes his shoulder. He begins to stir. Through thick lips he murmurs, "Rachel?"

"I'm here, Sam," she says.

He lifts his hand in an attempt to touch her, but it falls to the bed.

"He's out cold," Lou says. "You think she fooled him?"

"She would've fooled me," I say. "Except for the voice."

"The voice still needs work," Lou agrees. "But Hailey's good. She'll be ready when we need her."

"I'm counting on it."

Lou introduced me to Hailey Brimstone nine months ago. She was then—and continues to be—the best body double I've ever seen.

"Nice debut," I say.

"Sam was so drugged out, I doubt his conscious mind will remember seeing her."

Lou shook his head. "I hate dealing with geniuses. It's a hell of a lot easier beating normal people into cooperating."

"Yeah, but it wouldn't be as much fun."

We watch Hailey leave the room with Dr. Drake.

I ask, "Does Dr. Drake think Hailey's his wife?"

"Yes, of course."

"Good."

Lou and I watch the medical personnel enter the room. He says, "Do you feel bad about Sam's leg?"

"No."

"You're a hard case, Donovan."

"I gave him several chances to help me. And he refused."

"But you still need him."

"I do. But he needs to know I mean business."

"I expect this will convince him."

"You'd think so."

Two orderlies and two nurses transfer Sam to a gurney. Then they push him out the door, to surgery.

21.

IT'S LATE AFTERNOON, and Rachel has been gone five days and approximately twelve hours.

I spend the next two hours running the perimeter of the Sensory Resources complex, which is far and away the most beautiful running course I've ever seen. I'd describe it in detail if I had the time, but I don't. Because after a quick shower I get to my desk just as Sam is regaining consciousness for the second time. Deputies Caruso and Brightside are standing at his bedside. A nurse stands on the opposite side of Sam's bed, taking a reading of his vital signs. Some words were exchanged between Dr. Drake and the detectives a few moments earlier, the result being that Drake refused to allow the detectives access to Sam without a staff member being present.

Thirty minutes ago they had to administer a sedative after showing Sam his stump.

A few minutes pass, then Sam begins moaning.

"You've had a rough day," Detective Brightside says.

Sam looks at him. Then looks at Detective Caruso.

"Donovan Creed did this to me," he says.

"Who's Donovan Creed?" Brightside says.

"The guy with the snake. The guy who turned off my alarm. The guy who's trying to force me to tell him about Rachel."

"Rachel's your wife."

"Yes. Is she still here?"

"I don't know. We just got here a half-hour ago. She hasn't been in your room, though. And according to the nurses, you've had no visitors except us."

"She was here. I saw her. Spoke to her."

"Well, it's possible she got past the nurses. So what did Rachel do?"

"What do you mean?"

"You said this guy, Creed, is trying to force you to tell him about Rachel. What did she do, and why does he care?"

"She's been kidnapped."

The Genes look at each other. Caruso says, "You just said she was here."

Sam looks confused. "I must've dreamed it."

Caruso says, "What's this about a kidnapping? Did you dream that, too?"

"No. She was kidnapped."

"By who?"

"Whom."

"What?"

"By whom."

"That's what I'm askin'you, you prick."

Sam looks at Caruso. "What happened to your eyebrows?"

"What do you mean?"

Sam focuses on Brightside. "Last time you guys were here, his eyebrows were gone. Now yours are."

Brightside and Caruso look at each other. Brightside says, "Maybe we should come back after the drugs wear off. You're not making much sense."

"Do you have eyebrows or don't you?" Sam says.

"I don't," Brightside says. "But I haven't had eyebrows for three days. Gene's always had eyebrows, long as I've known him."

"That doesn't make sense," Sam says, looking back and forth from one Gene to the other. To Brightside, he says, "What happened to them?"

"What do you care?"

"I have to know."

Brightside shrugs. "My wife caught me cheating. We had a big fight, I got drunk, passed out on the couch. She shaved them off while I was unconscious. What's your story?"

"What do you mean?"

Brightside asks the nurse if she has a mirror.

"Top drawer," she says.

Caruso opens the drawer on the bed table, pulls out a hand mirror, holds it in front of Sam's face.

"What the fuck?"

"Guess we both got caught cheating, huh?" Brightside says.

Sam looks at the nurse. "Why the hell did you people shave my eyebrows?"

She says, "You've had no eyebrows since you've been here."

"*Creed!*" Sam shouts.

"You think this Creed character forced a snake to bite your nuts, then snuck into your hospital room and shaved off your eyebrows?" Brightside says.

"No. I think he shaved them off after the snake bit me. While I was lying on the floor, helpless."

Caruso frowns. "What kind of twisted fuck would do that?"

"The kind who'd let them amputate my leg to get what he wants."

"And what's that?" Brightside says.

"Rachel."

"What, he's after your wife?"

"He's her boyfriend. They've been having an affair for years."

"And someone kidnapped her? When?"

"He said Tuesday morning. Around the time the doctor died."

"What doctor?"

Sam shakes his head, trying to clear it. "Forget the doctor. A branch of the government sent a squad to kidnap Rachel. Creed's trying to find her. He came to me for help."

"What can you do?"

"I can logically deduce answers to hypothetical questions based on random bits of data."

Caruso says, "Give me a for instance."

"You want a for instance? Fine. I can tell you're not married."

"What, because I don't wear a ring?"

"No. Because you're uglier than shit."

"Asshole."

Brightside says, "What's the question Creed wants answered?"

Sam says, "Why would the government kidnap a woman and kill her doctor because of the results of her blood test?"

"So the doctor was killed?"

"I don't know."

"You said he was dead. Was he killed?"

"Creed thinks so."

Brightside nods. "We can check it out."

No one says anything for a minute. Then Brightside says, "Do you know?"

"What?"

"The answer to Creed's question."

Sam nods.

"What is it?"

At my desk, I lean forward.

22.

"GET RID OF the camera," Sam says.

"What camera?" Brightside says.

"The one Creed's monitoring us on."

"You think he snuck in here and put cameras in your room?"

"I know he did."

"When?"

"Before I got here."

Brightside frowns. "How would he know which room you'd get?"

"How the fuck do I know? He just does this shit. He can do anything. Trust me, he's watching us right now. *You hear that, Creed? I'm onto you!*" Sam shouts.

Brightside says, "That's crazy."

But Gene Caruso doesn't think so. He's looking around the room.

I'm not concerned. These are pinhole cameras, state of the art. They perfectly match the background. You'd have to know exactly what you're looking for and where to look.

Caruso picks up the chair from the corner and drags it to the far wall that faces the foot of Sam's bed.

"Sir—" the nurse says.

Caruso dismisses her with a wave of his hand. He climbs on the chair and stares straight into the camera.

"Nothing here," he says.

Then he pulls off his shoe and smashes the camera.

"*Sir!*" the nurse shouts.

My screen goes dead. Good thing I've got another one. The nurse presses the call button.

"What's that all about?" Brightside says.

"Son of a bitch was right. Pinhole camera. Smallest one I ever saw. Smaller than Sam's dick, even."

"Funny," Sam says. "There's got to be at least three more. Check every wall."

The nurse's station answers the page. Sam's nurse says, "The detectives need to leave. Please call security."

To the detectives, the nurse says, "I suggest you both leave. Immediately."

"We're conducting an investigation," Brightside says.

Caruso is busy checking the second wall.

"Nothing here," he says.

Brightside says, "Sam. Do you know where your wife is? Yes or no?"

I can't see Sam's face. But I hear him say, "No."

"So you don't know if she's been kidnapped at all."

"I believe him. About this."

"You say this happened on Tuesday? That's four days ago. Why wasn't it reported?"

"Rachel lives in seclusion with a lady named Nadine Crouch. She's a psychiatrist. When they kidnapped Rachel, they tried to kill Nadine. She's been in the hospital ever since. She was the only one who could've reported the kidnapping. And she was in a coma until yesterday. When she woke up, she called Creed."

"Why would she call him instead of you?"

"Because he's the one who employs her."

"Nothing on the third wall," Caruso says, which leaves the wall where my remaining camera is located. Caruso slides the chair over, and stands on it. He's about ten feet from my camera. He steps off the chair and slides it three feet closer. Then stands on it and carefully inspects the wall.

"What's the answer to the question?" Brightside says.

Caruso moves his chair to the edge of the bed. He has to stand almost three feet from the wall, because of the bed table. From that angle there's no way he can see my camera.

"I found it!" he yells.

He removes his shoe.

Two men from hospital security burst through the door. "Sir!" one of them says. "Step down!"

Gene Caruso puts his left hand against the wall to steady himself. His shoe is in his right hand. All I can see on my monitor is the bottom of his shoe as he's about to smack the camera.

"What's the answer?" Brightside says.

"Sir, stand *down!*" the guard says to Caruso.

Caruso ignores him. He winds up, ready to smash the camera.

Sam says, "Break the camera and I'll tell you."

Caruso's shoe smashes into the wall, bursting the camera.

But not the sound system. That's working fine. I hear Sam laughing. He calls me a prick.

Brightside and Caruso are talking to the nurse and guards. They're showing credentials. After a couple of minutes of discussion, the guards decide they don't have the power to throw the detectives out, because they're investigating a kidnapping, and Sam corroborates that fact.

Sam says, "If I tell you, you've got to promise not to talk to Creed."

"Why would we do that?" Brightside says.

"He'll get it out of you. But you can't tell him. You've got to tell your superiors. Promise me."

"Promise you what?" Brightside says.

"Promise you'll call your superiors from this room, before you leave."

"Fine."

"Say it."

"I promise."

"Caruso," Sam says, "guard the door. Creed will probably burst in here any second. I'll tell you guys, and no one else."

I don't know if the nurse is still there or not. But Sam speaks.

"Spanish flu, 1918," he says.

"What about it?" Brightside says.

"Don't you see? She's got the gene!"

"What gene?"

"Call your superiors. Tell them what I just said."

"I'm not sure what I'm supposed to tell them."

"Hurry! Before Creed gets here! He'll kill us all! Call your superiors! Tell them Rachel Case's blood contains the gene that can cure the Spanish flu!"

"Of 1918?" Brightside says. "Sam. Do you know what year this is?"

"Call them, you moron! Call them now! You promised."

I hear Brightside sigh. "Fine," he says. "I'll call them."

23.

MY PHONE RINGS.

Brightside says, "Sir, Rachel Case is—"

"I heard," I say. "I'm on my way."

I walk a hundred yards to the Sensory Resources hospital room where Sam has been staying since the snakebite. When I walk through the door, Sam says, "Fuck you all."

"What's all this about the Spanish flu?" I say.

Sam looks defeated. "Fuck you," he says, though he says it with very little emotion. I can see he's starting to shut down, mentally.

"Come on, Sam. Rachel's in trouble. Talk to me."

"You bastard! They cut off my *leg!*"

"You're making such a fuss about it. A word to the wise, Sam. No one likes a whiner."

"Oh, like *you* wouldn't complain?" Sam says. He grabs the sheet, throws it off of him. He wants me to see that his leg ends at the knee.

"Sam, your leg is fine."

"What?"

"That's not your leg."

Sam looks down at the heavily bandaged stump.

"Not my leg? Are you insane?"

He stares at Brightside. His head is moving very slightly, from side to side. He's thinking of something. Or replaying something in his mind. Finally he says, "You gave me a clue."

Brightside stands there quietly.

"Your father," Sam says.

"What about him?"

"First time we met. You said they named the hospital after him."

"So?"

Sam laughs a derisive laugh. "You dumb fuck. You don't even know."

"Know what?" Brightside says.

"The script Creed gave you. You didn't even get it. That's why I didn't pick up on it."

"What're you talking about?"

"The script called for you to say your father's name was Robin Brightside."

"So?"

"So you're Robin's son. And he's Caruso. Robinson Caruso." Sam shakes his head. "And I got snakebit on Friday, no less. I'm a moron."

"Don't be so hard on yourself," I say. "You were bitten by a water moccasin, after all."

"Twice."

"No, just once. On the ass."

Sam gestures to his stump.

I nod to Caruso. He holds the hand mirror away from the bed, so Sam can see how his leg is hanging down under it.

"They never cut your leg off," I say.

I rip the bandages off the end of his knee, where he thought his leg ended.

"There's a hole in your bed. I had them numb the bottom half of your leg. It's propped on a footstool beneath your bed. Your leg is fine. You just can't feel it. Now help me find Rachel."

Sam is so relieved he doesn't know what to do. But what he says is, "How do I know that's my leg? Maybe it's my leg, but it's not attached. You could've done anything to me."

"We could've avoided all this if you'd cooperated with me in the first place."

"You went to this much trouble?" Sam said.

"Rachel means the world to me."

"Who was the girl?"

"What girl?"

"The one who looked like Rachel. The one who came in my room."

"You must have dreamt that part."

"Get Dr. Drake. He'll tell me the truth."

"There is no Drake. He had to leave. He's performing *On the Waterfront* tonight at the little theater."

Caruso yells, "Stella! Stella!"

Sam says, "Where am I?"

"I can't disclose that."

"Give me a hint."

"When we put you under, it will require a plane flight to get you back to Louisville."

"How long a flight?"

"Don't even think I would tell you that."

"No problem. I'll just look up every town in America that has a little theater and narrow it down by the shows they're putting on."

"Sounds like a great project."

Sam looks at me. "You lied about the little theater."

"It was a figure of speech. I just meant he was an actor."

"Is he here or not?"

"Not."

Sam says, "Fine. I give up. Go save Rachel, if you can. You'll

97

probably die trying, and I'm fine with that."

"On the other hand, if I fail, you'll never see her again."

"She doesn't want to see me anyway."

"True. But if I bring her back, you'll still have hope."

Sam shrugs. Then says, "If you can prove that's my leg under the bed, and if it's attached to my knee, and if it works, and if you promise to let me go...I'll tell you what I know."

24

WE'RE IN SAM'S hospital room. I'm standing bedside, Lou's sitting on the hard-back chair, taking notes. Sam's sitting on a hospital bed that has no hole in it. His leg is propped up, and he's beginning to get some feeling below the knee, which causes his upper thigh to twitch.

Addressing me like a high-school professor lectures his students, Sam says, "What's the greatest threat to the world?"

I answer, "Nuclear weapons?"

"No."

"Terrorism?"

"No."

"Religious fanatics?"

"No."

"Politicians? Saturated fat? Oprah Winfrey?"

"Pandemic flu," Sam says.

"Do tell," I say.

"In 1918, in the space of three months, more than 40 million people died from the Spanish flu. But it was a misnomer."

"Why's that?" I ask.

"Because it started in Kansas."

"People die every year from the flu."

"Not this type. It never happened before, never happened since. It was, quite simply, the worst plague in the history of the world."

"Never heard of it," I said.

"Then you're a moron," Sam says.

I shrug. "At least I've got eyebrows."

Sam sighs. "Some of your stunts are so juvenile, I'm surprised you didn't put a tack in my chair."

"What made the flu of 1918 so bad?" I say.

Sam frowns. "Do you even know how the flu gets started each year?"

"In cold weather, people start coughing on each other and spread their colds. As more people get sick, the cold virus mutates into the flu, right?"

"You've got to be shitting me. Are you that stupid?"

"Pretend I am," I say, "and answer the question. Or I'll hit you with a spitball."

Sam shakes his head in disgust. He's convinced I'm completely beneath him intellectually. Since everyone else in the world shares that position, I could care less. I just want to find Rachel. He says, "The short answer why it was so bad: this is the only virus in history that killed the youngest and strongest people. It was also the most contagious. From start to finish, it lasted twenty-seven months. During that time one out of every three people in the world caught it, and 100 million of them died. As for how it started," Sam says, "I'll have to give you a simplified explanation. I'll be sure to use small words so you can keep up."

"You're very considerate. I've always said that about you."

Ignoring me, Sam continues: "Most animals that get the flu, get it from birds."

"Birds."

"That's right."

"Well, I've heard of bird flu," I say.

"Humans rarely catch flu directly from birds," Sam says. "The birds infect pigs, and pigs infect people."

"I've heard of swine flu, also."

"You and every third-grader. Look, do you want this explanation or not?"

"Me want!"

He says, "Every year, wild ducks migrate south for the winter."

"So?"

"One out of every three have the flu. Their droppings land in fields, streams, and lakes. They pass the flu on to pigs, and the farmers catch it. This happens all over the world around the same time each year. It also happens in Asia, where millions of chickens pass the flu on to pigs, who pass it on to humans. When people are infected with the flu virus, it spreads as they come into contact with other people."

"If this happens every year, why was 1918 worse?"

"Pigs have both avian and human flu receptors, so they can catch the flu from birds *and* people. Scientists believe that in the spring of 1918, a pig caught a human strain of flu from a person, then caught an avian strain from a wild duck. Every known flu virus is made up of eight gene segments. But the 1918 strain was a mix of eight from the human, eight from the bird, and eight from the pig, creating a lethal hybrid the world had never seen. As it spread, it continued to mutate, becoming more and more lethal. It was wartime, and infected soldiers from Kansas were deployed to bases and battlefields all over the world. As the Kansas flu strain mixed with the flu strains from other countries, the virus continued to mutate exponentially. By the time it hit Spain it was so deadly they called it the Spanish flu. And it's been called that, ever since."

I hold up my hand. "You mean to tell me that because a

single pig in Kansas ate some duck shit one morning, 100 million people died?"

"Yes. That's what I'm saying. In general."

"And what's all this got to do with Rachel?"

"Every year the World Health Organization hosts a meeting among the top scientists in the world, and public health officials, to determine if the Spanish flu could return that year."

"I've never heard of that."

"I'm not surprised. But you're not alone. Even newspapers and textbooks in the years that followed the pandemic barely mention the flu of 1918."

"Why not?"

"I don't know. Nor do I know why kids aren't taught about it in history. Maybe they don't want to cause a panic. But what I *do* know is the world is smaller now than it was in 1918. And every year it's more likely the Spanish flu will return. And when it does, it's going to wipe out a third of the Earth's population."

"You still haven't told me what Rachel's blood test has to do with this."

"Pull up a chair," Sam says, "because here's where it gets interesting."

"I hope to hell it does," I say, "because if I wrote all this in a book, my readers would be snoring by now."

25.

"THERE IS NO cure for the Spanish flu," Sam says. "And scientists can't make a vaccine for it, because the live virus has only been seen twice. The first was in 1995, at Walter Reed Army Medical Center, when a researcher found a preserved tissue sample from a Spanish flu victim who died 77 years earlier. Unfortunately, that sample was taken from a soldier who died before the flu mutated into the deadliest form."

"I thought you said this was getting interesting," I say.

"By the end of 1918 the flu had spread throughout the world," Sam says, "including Alaska. In 1997 a scientist found the body of a young woman he and some Eskimo helpers dug out of the permafrost. The flu-causing agent was still in her lungs. They've tried to isolate and identify the genetic code for that strain ever since."

"So?"

"I think they found it."

"So why can't they create a vaccine?"

"If I'm right, they lack a live strand of genetic code that contains a natural receptor to the exact form of the virus that wiped out all those millions of people. They've got the wild duck and pig strains isolated. But the chances of finding the perfect human genetic match are...impossible to one."

"But somehow Rachel has it?"

"That's my guess," Sam says.

"I always said Rachel was one in a million."

"This would make her one in six billion."

"And they've what, checked every blood sample in the world every day until they finally found the receptor gene in hers?"

"For the last five years. In developed countries, anyway."

"But how?"

"Computer analysis."

"Wouldn't every doctor or blood-lab tech be able to recognize it?"

"Not if they don't know what to look for. It would show up as an anomaly. No one is going to read the results and say, 'Aha!'"

"Except the scientists who know what to look for."

"That's right. Most people would look at Rachel's blood test results and think the sample had been contaminated."

"So why kill her doctor? Why try to kill Nadine? Why kidnap Rachel?"

"You mean, why not just ask her to donate enough blood to start creating a vaccine?"

"Exactly."

"Think of the implications for bioterrorism. What would happen if word got out that Rachel was the missing link to the deadliest virus the world has ever known?"

"I suppose all sorts of good and evil people would be clamoring to kidnap her and harvest her receptor gene."

"Yes, but the bad guys could also inoculate themselves against the flu, and unleash it on the rest of the world."

"Holy shit!"

"I told you it was interesting."

"So you think our government kidnapped her and is holding her somewhere to harvest her blood?"

"At the very least."

"What's that mean?"

"If you were the government, what would you do?" Sam says.

"Raise taxes?"

"Funny. They can't take a chance on her dying. So they'll take as much blood as they can, freeze it, and harvest her eggs, create children who will continue supplying them with genetic code."

"They want Rachel's children?"

"That would be my guess."

"How much blood do they need?"

"To inoculate the world? Every year? I have no idea, but it's probably more than any twenty people could provide. How much blood is required to yield a single proper genetic strand? I don't know. But it's a lot, because they'll have to combine the proper strand from a duck, a pig, and a human. And even though they've isolated the proper components, the flu is an RNA virus."

"You mean DNA?"

"No. DNA has double strands of genetic code, RNA has just one."

"So?"

"RNA is highly unstable, and breaks down in hours, not days."

"If they get the right combination, how do they make the vaccine?"

"They have to create the actual Spanish flu virus in the lab. Then culture it in eggs."

"Rachel's eggs?"

"No, chicken eggs, you dolt."

He sighs at my stupidity, then continues. "They inject a

minute portion of the live virus into a chicken egg. After a few days, that creates maybe a teaspoon of vaccine. It will take millions of gallons to create enough vaccine to inoculate the world, and they have to do it one egg at a time."

"That would take forever."

"Not one egg then a second one," Sam says. "They start with a few hundred, then a few thousand, then tens of thousands at a time. It involves time and people. And millions of chicken eggs. And money, and resources. And that's just for one flu season. And only if the Spanish flu turns up that year. In other words, they won't start producing the vaccine until they know they need it."

"They'd go to all that trouble for something they won't even use?"

"No. They'd go to all that trouble if the Spanish flu comes back. And they'll keep Rachel locked up until that happens. And if it doesn't happen in her lifetime, they'll have her offspring on hand in case that strain of flu breaks out in their lifetimes."

"You're telling me that someone plans to create children and lock them up as lifetime blood donors for a flu vaccine that only occurs when a human infects a pig who gets infected by a duck who reinfects the human?"

"By George, I think you've got it!" Sam says.

"Yeah, that sounds like a government project," I say. "But no one is going to lock up Rachel's kids. Not on *my* watch."

Sam laughs. "Like there's a lot *you* can do about it. If I'm right, Rachel has just become the most important person in the world. They'll have her locked up so tight the president himself won't be able to find her. I bet there aren't five people in the world who know where she is."

Lou and I exchange a look.

Sam says, "How could you possibly locate her?"

"By locating those who need her."

He frowns. "If you *do* find her, how could you possibly hope to rescue her?"

"I'll find a way. Trust me on that."

Sam says, "You're insane."

"In my line of work, being insane is a plus."

Sam shakes his head. "Even if you find her, and rescue her, where could you possibly go? How could you keep the world from finding you?"

"I haven't worked that part out yet. But tell me this: how much would a vaccine like that be worth?"

"Shut up."

"That much, huh?"

"There is no sum too high to demand."

"A zillion dollars?" I say.

"There's no such number."

"All the riches of the world?"

"Beyond what it takes to run the world, yes."

"Sounds like a zillion dollars to me," I say.

"Are you done with me?" Sam says. "If we're through, I'd like to go home now."

"First, let's figure out who would be in charge of creating the vaccine."

"Some drug company. Or companies."

"American, I presume, because of security issues. American companies that have experience creating large quantities of flu vaccine. That's got to be a small number, wouldn't you think?"

"Less than a half-dozen, probably." He looks at me. "What

are you planning to do?"

"Save Rachel's children."

"She doesn't have any children, you idiot."

"And I'm going to keep it that way."

"You truly are insane."

26.

IT'S A LOT easier to kill someone than kidnap them.

Especially if you're working alone.

But what's easier still is breaking into their home while they're away, and waiting till they return.

Sam wants to hurry back to his strange life in Louisville, but I'm keeping him locked up at Sensory in case I want to test the accuracy of the comments I expect to get from the people I plan to visit. It's good for Sam to stay there another night anyway, since he hasn't fully recovered from the nip he got on the ass.

According to the information Lou dug up for me, Quentin Palmer heads the flu Division of the Center for Disease Control. I don't know if Quentin can help, but since he lives a scant hour from Sensory Resources, he's a convenient place to start.

It's 6:00 p.m., Sunday, and I'm in one of Sensory's nondescript cars, driving through Quentin's stately neighborhood. These aren't multi million-dollar estates, but they're expensive, sprawling, older homes with ancient oaks and mature pine. I stop a hundred feet from Quentin's two-story, bleached stone home. The house itself looks sturdy, but the roof needs attention. The red shingles are faded and there's evidence of dry rot. I stare at the roof a moment, searching for the word that best describes it. The one that comes to mind is tired.

Quentin Palmer's roof is tired. It's done its job, but remains there stoically, unappreciated, fighting the elements bravely, like an old prizefighter who'd quit if he could, but he needs the money.

Quentin's house sits on three unkempt acres. As I'm viewing it, the garage door suddenly starts to rise, and I see a navy Escalade backing out. I put my car in gear and drive past the house, make the block, and keep moving until I find a "For Sale" sign, which turns out to be a quarter-mile from Quentin's house. I turn into that driveway and stop in front of the garage doors. After verifying no one's home, I walk to Quentin's house.

I hadn't been able to tell if the whole family—dad, mom, and Shelby—had been in Quentin's Escalade, but it's dinner time, so it's likely they were all heading out for a bite together. I didn't have a formal plan, but figured to stage a home invasion, tie the wife and daughter up, and rapidly beat some information out of Quentin. After all the crap Sam put me through, I was looking forward to a more straightforward method of getting answers.

I'm quite skilled at breaking and entering, but right now I don't feel like being subtle. Like Quentin's roof, I'm tired. Tired of dealing with Sam's bullshit, tired of dealing with the government, tired of worrying about Rachel. I feel like kicking the door down. Since the Palmers' back door is completely secluded from the neighbors, and since the closest neighbors are more than fifty yards away, I decide to kick it just right of the deadbolt, and take my chances the Palmers don't have a burglar alarm. Or if they do, it's not set. But then I remember reading somewhere that twelve percent of all families fail to check the doors and windows before going out to dinner. I don't know if that's true, but it's worth the effort to see. I try the door knob and—no big surprise—it's locked. I go around to the side and find the sliding door unlocked. Score one for the article. And one for me as well, because the house is silent. Meaning, if they do have a burglar alarm, it wasn't set.

A minute later, I learn why.

"Thought you were having dinner with your family," I say, turning the corner and finding Quentin Palmer sitting at his desk.

Quentin jumps to his feet. "Wh—Who are you? What's the meaning of this? What do you want?"

I enter his office. Quentin is very nervous.

"Please," I say. "Have a seat."

"I'm not a wealthy man," he says. "Whatever you might think, we're barely making ends meet."

"Really?"

"It's true. I swear."

"Why's that, do you think? I know you earn a good wage."

He turns his palm up and gestures meekly, indicating not just the room we're in, but his life in general. "My wife lost her job last year. The house is eating us alive. Private school tuition, car payments, college on the horizon…" Quentin shakes his head.

"How can I help?" I say.

"Excuse me?"

"Sounds like you're in crisis. How much cash would it take to get you through this tough time in your life?"

Quentin takes a seat at his desk. He's still concerned, but now he's confused, as well.

"Aren't you here to rob me?" he says.

"Do I look like a thief?"

"A little."

I frown, and point to one of the chairs facing his desk.

"May I?"

He nods.

"If you don't mind, I'm going to slide this chair to the side. That way I can see if anyone tries to sneak up behind me."

"There's no one home but me," he says.

"You were surprisingly quiet," I say.

He looks at his computer. "I get wrapped up in my work."

"Actually, that's why I'm here, Quentin. To discuss your work."

"I don't understand."

I open his printer tray and remove a sheet of paper. "Got an ink pen?" I ask.

He starts to open his desk drawer. I say, "Freeze!"

He does.

"I doubt you have a gun in there, but I'd feel ridiculous if you shot me."

I get up, push his chair back, and check the drawers. As I suspected, there's no gun. No knives, either. Or throwing stars, nunchucks or water moccasins. I do find a pen, and hand it to him.

"What's this about?" he says.

"I want you to write some names for me. Specifically, the name of each and every drug company that manufactures flu vaccine."

"Are you serious?"

"Do I look serious?"

He looks at me. "Yes."

"Then do it."

"Well, I know many of them, of course, but not all. The big companies use subcontractors for some of the work. Knowing the names of these companies doesn't fall under my job description. But none of this information is secret. It's a matter of public record. Anyone with a computer can obtain it."

"I know that, Quentin. I'm starting slowly, building a rapport. Trying to create a bond with you. Of sorts."

"I appreciate that," he says.

He writes down the names of seven companies before I stop him.

"That's good enough."

He hands me the sheet. I already know these names. "You're doing fine," I say. "Now I want you to answer six very important questions."

Quentin can tell by my tone I'm expecting complete candor. He swallows. "I'll be fully cooperative," he says.

"Glad to hear it. Question number one: have you ever heard of the Spanish flu of 1918?"

He looks at me curiously. "Yes, of course."

"Good. That's a throwaway question. Here's number two: has a vaccine been invented that could prevent the Spanish flu from coming back?"

"No."

Quentin is relaxing a bit, though I have no idea why.

"Question three: look at me." He does. "Look directly into my eyes, and do not look away when I ask you this next question. Do you understand?"

He looks into my eyes and holds my stare. Then says, "Yes, sir."

27.

"QUESTION NUMBER THREE is, what's your wife's bra size?"

"Excuse me?"

"That was another throwaway question. It's from a book I read. Question number four: how close is this country, or any country, to developing a vaccine for the Spanish flu?"

"It can't be done."

"And why is that?"

"Such a vaccine would require a human genetic footprint that doesn't exist."

"Why not?—And by the way, these ancillary questions aren't part of the six."

"Do you know much about synthetic biology?"

"Pretend I don't."

"There is no known human genetic code that can recreate the virus that caused the pandemic, though some scientists are working with man-made cells that get genetic instructions from a synthetic DNA."

I hold up my hand. "Call on me."

Quentin furrows his brow. "Excuse me?"

"When I was a kid, in class, I'd raise my hand and the teacher would call on me. I'm raising my hand, Quentin."

"I'm afraid I don't understand."

"Call on me."

"I—I don't know your name."

"That's right, you don't. Just like I don't know what the shit you're talking about."

"Perhaps if I—"

"Let me make this simple, Quentin. Suppose there was a human who had the proper genetic code. A lady. Where would you hide her?"

"Hide her?"

"It's a simple question."

"Why would I hide her?"

"Because you don't want the bad guys to get her."

Quentin looks concerned again. "Your questions are making me uncomfortable. I'm concerned you might be unstable."

"Question number five, rephrased: if the government found this lady, where would they hide her?"

"I don't know anything about a lady. What lady are you talking about?"

"Rachel Case."

"I've never heard the name. I honestly know nothing about her."

"Rachel is in her late twenties. She has thick, light brown, shoulder-length hair with blonde highlights. Her lips aren't full, but they aren't thin, either. But when she smiles...No, strike that. Not *when* she smiles, but *after*."

"I beg your pardon?"

"After Rachel rewards you with a smile, her lips curl up at the edges, turning her mouth into a little bow."

"A bow?"

"It's adorable."

"I'm sure it is, but—"

"Her eyes."

"Her…eyes?"

"Gold, like tupelo honey. And her breath?

"Yes?"

"I don't care what she's eaten, or how long it's been since she brushed her teeth. Her breath is always fresh. Like the negative ions in the air after a spring storm washes over a field of honeysuckle. Have you ever known a woman to have that type of breath?"

"No."

"Damn right you haven't. And her perfect breath dances behind teeth as pure and white as the 3,617 words Melville used in Chapter 42 to describe how white the whale was. And Rachel's body?"

"Yes?"

"Whippet thin. Willowy. With small, splendid breasts and nipples hard as cherry stones. A belly so firm and flat you could use it to crack walnuts."

"Walnuts?"

"And legs that go on forever. Impossibly well-proportioned legs. Do you understand what I'm trying to say, Quentin?"

"She has nice legs."

"No. Supermodels have nice legs. Rachel's alabaster thighs will send you howling through the night as you bound across the moors, seeking your very sanity. As for what beckons in the golden-tufted triangle atop those splendid thighs, well, that's none of your business."

"Of course not."

"But I'll say this much, Quentin: as a mysterious force of nature that will spin your compass, render all navigation useless, and swallow you whole, the Bermuda Triangle has nothing on Rachel's triangle. Add to that a backside that would make even the most devoted husband in the world curse his wedding vows."

"She sounds extraordinary."

"Damn right, she is. And I want her back."

Quentin's cell phone buzzes on his desk. I pick it up and look at the caller ID.

"Who's Ginger?"

"My wife. She's calling from the restaurant. I'm supposed to join them for dinner."

I set the phone back on his desk.

"Don't answer it," I say.

"If I don't, she'll worry."

"She'll worry more if you're dead. And you will be, if you answer it."

"She'll keep calling."

"How would you feel if someone kidnapped Ginger?"

"Sir…"

"Would you miss her?"

"Of course, but—"

"What would you do to get her back?"

"I'd do anything. But—"

I stand. "Where do you keep your tools? In the garage?"

"My tools?"

"Let's go find them."

"Wh—Why?"

"Because my last question might require some coaxing."

28.

I WAS WRONG.

My last question required practically no coaxing.

I'm glad, because the bottom line is Quentin's a standup guy. A caring husband, good father, the sort of man you want looking after your nation when flu season strikes.

"You're not going to leave me like this, are you?" he says, as I open the door that leads from his shop to the house proper.

"Ginger will let you out," I say, as I start to leave. "By the way, where's your checkbook?"

"I—I thought you weren't going to rob me."

"I need a deposit slip."

"Why?"

"So I can wire you some money."

"I'd rather you just left us alone."

I look at Quentin, bent over his workbench, hands tied behind his back, his head stuck in the vice, and smile. "Don't be a martyr. We all need help. By the way, I'm counting on you not to tell anyone about our visit. Not Ginger, and especially not Maggie Sullivan."

"How will I explain having my head stuck in a vice?"

"To Ginger and Shelby?"

"Yes."

"Tell them it was an accident."

"An accident?"

"I'm really concerned that you're going to report this to someone. Normally I'd kill you, and that would be that. But you seem a decent man. I'm hoping I can trust you to keep your word."

"You can."

"But now you're making me wonder. If I leave you here, Ginger might demand to know how you got into this position. If I cut you loose, I'll have to trust you not to call the police, or warn Maggie Sullivan's office that I'm coming to call."

"I give you my word."

I sigh, walk back to Quentin, and untie his hands. "Don't make me sorry I'm doing this," I say. "Because the smart move is to kill you."

"I won't say a word."

"I'm going to trust you. Against my better judgment. Knowing that if you tell anyone, I'm going to do something I really don't want to do."

"What's that?"

I take out my cell phone, punch in some numbers, and set it on speaker.

"Yes?"

"Callie, I've got you on speaker phone."

"Okay."

"I'm with Quentin Palmer. He gave me a name. Maggie Sullivan."

"World Health Organization Maggie Sullivan?"

"The same."

"He's going to call her in a few minutes and get me an appointment to see her tomorrow."

"I'm what?" Quentin says. "I barely know her!"

Callie says, "Will Maggie know where Rachel is?"

"Probably not. But she'll know the name of the scientist who gave the green light on Rachel's blood work."

To Quentin, I say, "I'll need you to call Maggie before I leave."

"It's Sunday."

"You'd prefer I spend the night with your family?"

"No!"

"Then you'll have to make the call in a few minutes."

"I don't have her home phone number."

"Try her cell."

Quentin turns the palms of both hands upward in frustration. "She and I don't have that type of relationship?"

"What type is that?"

"The type where I can call her on a Sunday evening and ask her to see someone the next day."

"But that's the very reason she'll take it seriously, yes?"

"I'm not sure what I should say."

"We can rehearse a bit, before you call."

"You're not planning to put her head in a vice, are you?"

"Not unless I have to."

Callie is laughing on her end of the phone. "You put his head in a vice? That's hilarious!"

"Sounds funnier than it is," I say. "Callie, I've decided not to kill Quentin."

She pauses before saying, "Loose ends, Donovan."

"I know. But he's a good man. God knows, the country needs some."

"Still…"

"I know. Listen, do me a favor. Tell Quentin something to convince him we're serious."

"Shooting him would be more convincing."

"Humor me," I say.

120

"Quentin," Callie says. "Can you hear me?"

"Yes."

"36-C."

"Excuse me?"

"Ginger's bra size. Trust me, we know everything about her. And we know more about Shelby than you do."

"Can you give him a for instance?" I say.

"Shelby's dating Brad Ogilvie, senior at Mid-Central High, but she's crushing on Charlie Garber, a freshman at UVA. She started taking birth-control pills two months ago and has three left, if she's taken them according to the prescription. She bought two online tickets to the advance showing of *Follow the Stone*, which premieres next Friday."

"H—How do you people *know* these things?" Quentin says.

"It's our job to know them, Mr. Palmer," Callie says, adding, "And know this: if you say one word about this to anyone, your life will come to an end. The warning you give tonight or tomorrow might destroy the man standing beside you, but you don't even know who I am. And I'll come for you. And when I do, I'm going to cut Ginger and Shelby into cubes of chum, right before your eyes."

"Jesus," Quentin says.

"And you know what's worse?" Callie says.

"Wh—what?"

"I am so fucking depraved at this point, I will actually enjoy it."

"Jesus," I say.

29.

"WOULD YOU LIKE to see my shillelagh, Mr. Creed?"
Maggie Sullivan says.

"Well, I've never heard it called that before, but...should I lock the door?"

She laughs heartily. "You're a bad boy!"

"So you're not actually going to..."

"Of course not, you nut. A shillelagh is an Irish walking stick."

It's Monday afternoon. A week has passed since Rachel's kidnapping. I'm in Maggie Sullivan's office in Denver. After not killing Quentin Palmer, I had him contact Maggie to set up an appointment to discuss a possible breakthrough for a flu vaccine, though he was careful not to mention the Spanish flu. Maggie and I have been having fun talking about her Irish heritage. She's fifteen years older than me, and mildly flirtatious. She stands and crosses the room and removes a stick from a display on the far wall. She hefts it a couple of times before handing it to me.

"Mighty fine-looking shillelagh," I say.

She laughs again. "You have no idea what you're looking at, do you?"

"It sort of resembles an Irish walking stick," I say, handing it back. "What type of wood is that?"

"Like most traditional shillelaghs, this one is made from

blackthorn. You smear the wood with butter and put it up the chimney to cure."

"Are we speaking in code here?"

She laughs again.

I say, "It's heavy on top."

"Yes. This is what we call a loaded shillelagh. The top end has been hollowed and filled with molten lead, which turns it into a striking stick."

"Have you ever hit anyone with it?"

"No, but my grandmother claims to have used it to beat off the men in her neighborhood."

"My grandmother used her hand," I say.

"Excuse me?"

"Nothing. It's a nice walking stick."

"Yes, well it should be. It's an antique, after all. A classic, as it were."

"If I'm not mistaken, a jeweled shillelagh is given each year to the winner of the college football game between Notre Dame and USC."

She gives me a slow nod, then smiles. "You've been having sport with me all this time."

I return her smile. "Maybe. A little."

She says, "How can I help you, Mr. Creed?"

"By giving me a name."

"And which name would that be?"

"The head scientist. The one who has the final word."

She frowns. "I'm afraid I don't know what you're asking. Mr. Palmer said your visit had something to do with next year's flu vaccine."

"Please forgive my lack of scientific credentials as I try to formulate my question," I say, humbly.

"Of course."

"Suppose I had access to a human gene that was one in a billion."

Maggie shrugs.

I continue. "And let's say that the gene I've found is the missing link between the swine and avian flu strains that caused the Spanish flu pandemic of 1918."

"That would be quite a find," Maggie says.

"But assume it were true."

"Done, sir."

"If I had access to such a gene, who is the scientist that would validate my claim?"

"Roger Asprin."

"Asprin?"

"Yes, of course."

"That's quite a name," I say.

"Roger is the do-all and be-all of virologists, what we call a true 'flu man', meaning a scientist who has devoted his entire life to influenza research."

"If a determination needs to be made, he's the guy?"

"He's the one."

"He knows his stuff?"

"In addition to being the world's most highly respected virologist, Roger Asprin is a molecular pathologist with extensive experience in recovering genetic information from preserved human tissue."

I have no idea what she's talking about, but I call Sam and Lou and have her repeat Roger's credentials to them.

"Roger sounds like the man," Sam says.

"Where would I find Mr. Asprin?" I say.

Maggie laughs. "Roger's a man of the world. He could be anywhere. It would be easier to gain audience with the president."

I frown.

"However," she adds, "this week I happen to know he's in Chicago, heading a symposium on viral pathogens."

"Where's his home?"

"Los Angeles, I think."

I turn off the speaker phone and wait until Lou says, "Got it. Newport Beach."

When I terminate the call, Maggie says, "Tell me what you've found, Mr. Creed."

I then proceed to give Maggie the complete and utter bullshit story that Sam concocted for me, and as we expected, she quickly came to the conclusion that what I actually had was nothing. To her credit, she listened to the entire spiel before saying, "And you discussed all this with Quentin Palmer?"

"No. I only told him what he told you on the phone."

"And he didn't ask for details?"

"Yes, of course he did. But I didn't know if I could trust him, since he said he didn't know the name of the scientist."

Maggie nods. "Well, he's certainly heard of Roger Asprin. On the other hand, he'd have no reason to know Dr. Asprin is our primary accreditor."

"Can you help me get an audience with him?" I say, knowing the answer in advance.

"I'll see what I can do," Maggie says. "Though I must warn you, he's a very busy man."

"I'd appreciate any help you can give. After all, it would be horrible if the Spanish flu came back."

"It would indeed." She stood, and extended her hand. "I'll have someone from his office contact you."

"My number's on the business card I gave you," I say, helpfully.

She picks the card up and looks at it. "So it is."

I shake her hand and give her a wink. "Thanks for showing me your shillelagh."

"Anytime, Mr. Creed."

I leave her office knowing my card will be in her trash can before I hit the elevator button. Not that it matters, since the phone number I had printed on the card goes to a Chinese take-out restaurant in Richmond, Virginia.

I climb in my waiting limo and call Callie, who lives in Las Vegas with her girlfriend, Eva, a trapeze artist who performs nightly in the Cirque du Soleil production "O" at the Bellagio.

"I've just passed the city limits en route to Newport Beach," Callie says.

"Great! Thanks, Callie. I'll meet you there," I say. Then I call Lou and tell him to release Sam.

"Are you sure?"

"He gave us what we need. Plus, if all goes well tonight, we'll need his room at Sensory."

"Want me to fly him back to Louisville?"

"He's been through a lot. Take him wherever he wants to go. And Lou?"

"Yeah?"

"Thank him for me. I know he hates me, but I owe him big time. Without his help, I'd have no chance of finding Rachel."

"He didn't help you willingly," Lou reminds me.

"True. But the end result is the same."

Lou pauses a moment. Then says, "I'll take care of it."

30.

"ROGER'S IN CHICAGO till Friday," Jane Asprin says. "Some type of international conference."

"Then who's this?" I say, pointing my gun at the naked guy sitting on the bed beside her.

"I have no idea," Jane says. "A rapist, obviously. As you can see, he tied my wrists to the headboard and took off all my clothes. If you hadn't come in when you did, he would certainly have raped me."

"It didn't sound like rape," I say.

"You just walked in. Perhaps you didn't hear me calling for help."

"It didn't appear you needed any help. This guy came to your door, you let him in, called him Hector, and gave him five hundred dollars to tie you up."

"If you heard all that, why did you wait so long to barge in?"

"I didn't want to miss the show."

"You're disgusting." To Hector, she said, "Are you just going to sit there with your hands up your ass? Do something, you imbecile!"

"He's got a gun," Hector says.

Jane sighs. "At the very least you could untie me. You think it's fun lying here butt naked while some asshole points a gun at me? I can tell you this, Hector: a *real* man wouldn't *stand* for it."

Hector looks at me.

"No, you can't untie her," I say.

Hector looks at Jane. "He says—"

"I heard him." To me, she says, "Did Roger send you?"

"No."

"Are you going to tell him?"

"About what?"

"Hector."

"Do you *want* me to tell him?"

"What kind of crazy question is that? Of *course* not."

From behind me, Callie says, "I've got his laptop."

When she enters the room, Hector's eyes bug out like marbles. "*Firewood!*" he shouts, crossing himself.

I have no idea what that means.

Jane says, "Who *are* you people, movie stars gone bad?"

"What do *you* think?" I say.

As good-looking as I am synthetically, and Rachel is naturally, Callie has us both beat. She is, quite frankly, the most astonishingly beautiful woman in the world. In Jane's bedroom now, all three of us are staring at her.

"What?" Callie says.

"Your beauty."

"Oh, please. I look like a hairball some cat coughed up and shit on. Why is Jane still tied up? You can't possibly find her attractive."

I look at Jane's body a moment. "It's sort of like a movie you're not really into. But it's the only thing on TV, so you watch it."

"I'm right here, you know," Jane says.

"What's her version?" Callie says.

"She was telling me how Hector was about to rape her just now."

"Rehearsing her story for hubby?"

"I suppose."

Callie sets Roger's laptop on the floor and pulls her cell phone from the hip pocket of her jeans. She moves in close and takes Jane's picture from the waist up.

"What the *hell*?" Jane says.

Callie backs up a few steps and takes another photo, getting Jane's entire body in the shot. Then she shows me the digital images.

"What do you think?" she says.

"I think you did the best you could with what you had."

"Fuck you!" Jane says.

"Can't get enough, can she?" Callie says.

I tell Hector to get dressed.

"I don't have no underwear," he says, with great sorrow, as if apologizing.

Callie and I exchange a glance. We aren't sure, but we think Hector might be mentally challenged.

When Hector finally realizes he can get dressed the same way he got undressed, without underwear, I walk him downstairs, and out the door and tell him to go home. It's dark enough that I can probably get Jane's body into my trunk without anyone noticing. Hector tries to hug me goodbye, but I keep him at arm's length. I feel for the guy, but what can I say? I've got trust issues.

I close the door, lock it, and walk up the stairs. When I enter the bedroom, Jane says, "How long are you going to make me lie here naked?"

"I'm not sure. So far, I'm comfortable with it."

Callie is standing at the window, watching Hector walk away.

Jane says, "If you promise to let me go, I'll let you fuck

me." She looks at Callie and says, "Her, too."

Callie suddenly turns and runs out the door. "Start without me," she calls as she moves quickly down the steps.

When I hear the front door close behind her, my head explodes with pain.

31.

"WHERE'S JANE?" CALLIE asks, ten minutes later.

"In the trunk of my car."

"You drugged her?"

"Drugged and duct-taped. How's Hector?"

"Not so good. He was getting ready to call the cops."

"Not as impaired as we thought?"

"He seemed more lucid on the phone."

"Did he get through?"

"To the cops? No. But he spoke to his drug dealer."

"You're guessing he was going to call the cops?"

"Those were his last words before hanging up. He said, 'Gotta go, there's some strange shit goin'down. I might have to call the cops.'"

"He told his dealer he might call the cops?"

"He had the brains of a goldfish," Callie said. "But I don't think he was clinically mental."

I don't say anything to Callie about the white-hot pain that washed through my head for a split second, minutes ago. Once again, I feel fine almost instantly. But I'm a little concerned about driving through LA. If this thing flares up again, I could have a wreck.

"You going to follow me to the airport?" I ask.

Callie nods. Then asks, "What happened with Bernard?"

Bernard is a dean's list student at UCLA Medical. He's also

Jane and Roger's son.

"Jeff's got him in his trunk. He's currently making wide circles around the airport, waiting for us. He can take care of your car later tonight." Jeff is one of my former assassins who offered to pitch in for this project. Unlike Callie, Jarvis and me, Jeff actually lives in LA.

"What if Roger doesn't care we kidnapped his family?"

"I expect he's proud of Bernard. The kid's a top student, plans to follow in dad's footsteps. As a backup, Jarvis is still watching Ellen's house in Atlanta." Ellen is the Asprins' married daughter, and a new mom. Judging from the baby pictures on Roger's desk, he's quite fond of his granddaughter.

"You think that's enough?" Callie says.

"To get Rachel released? No."

"He'd let them all die?"

"I think so. He's a scientist. This thing with Rachel is a big deal."

"So what are you going to do?"

"What I do best."

"Remind me what that is," she says, smiling.

"I'm going to torture him."

"Can I watch?"

"But of course."

32.

WE'RE AIRBORNE. JANE and Bernard are comfortably sedated, and lying on the twin couches at mid-cabin. Callie and I are sitting aft, keeping an eye on them. If all goes according to plan, they won't wake up till they find themselves strapped to hospital beds in the Sensory Resources Medical Center.

Callie and I have the type of relationship where we're comfortable being silent for long periods of time when traveling together. She knows I'm upset about Rachel, but doesn't attempt to comfort or reassure me. I appreciate that about her. She doesn't like Rachel, and is far too honest to feign sympathy. She's only participating in this adventure as a favor to me, same as Jeff and Jarvis. Same as I'd drop everything to help them.

So I'm sitting here in silence, running the whole Rachel kidnapping through my mind, filtering it through Sam's theory about the flu pandemic of 1918, and can't help but think I'm missing something. There's a solution here, or at least a Plan B. I can *feel* it. I just can't see it.

I run it again, and still come up with nothing.

I quit trying to figure out what I'm missing, and decide instead to access some of my favorite memories of Rachel. In the attic of my mind there are many boxes labeled Rachel. Some say Rachel and Kevin, for that's the name I gave her when we met, and it's the name she's called me ever since. But each box holds a specific memory. I let my thoughts drift around the attic until I come to the box that says *First Time*. In my mind, I open that box, and find us riding horses across the lush Kentucky meadows on a crisp, spring day. She'd skipped work to be with me, and I'd found a gorgeous riding stable that agreed to rent me a couple of spirited horses for an afternoon picnic.

For weeks the sexual tension had been building between us, and after an hour of working the horses we found ourselves lying on the red-and-white-checked picnic blanket I'd brought for the occasion. We were in a secluded area, surrounded by a stand of pine trees, next to a bubbling brook. If it was ever going to happen, I figured, it would happen here. It was, quite simply, a perfect setting.

We had some lunch, shared some bourbon, and Rachel looked me dead in the eye, unbuttoned the top button of her shirt and said, "All day long you've been looking at my ass like it's your job."

"It *is* my job," I said.

She smiled. "Do you have any idea what I'm going to let you do to me right now?"

I smiled back. "Tell me."

"Nothing," she said.

"Nothing?"

"Nothing."

"Why?"

"I want our first time to be special."

I looked around, bewildered, unable to imagine a more romantic setting for our first time.

"What did you have in mind?" I said, utterly confused.

"When it's right, we'll both know it," she said.

I gave her a look.

"Don't pout," she said.

I gave her another look.

She kissed me. "Seriously, Kevin, I'm worth waiting for."

"I believe you."

She gestured with her arm at the setting around us. "This... is bullshit."

"Bullshit?"

"No offense."

"How could I possibly take offense?" I said, sarcastically.

She laughed. "You are so totally used to getting your way with women, aren't you?"

I shrugged.

"You've had prettier than me, I'm sure."

I said nothing.

"And smarter."

I still said nothing.

"And sweeter, and nicer, and cuter, and more romantic, and you know what?"

"What?"

"None of those things were enough for you."

I cocked my head and squinted a moment, and realized she was right. But before I had a chance to comment about it, she grabbed my crotch and cooed, "Wait till you see what I've got planned for Bullshit!"

"Bullshit?"

"That's what I'm going to call your manhood. I just decided."

"Surely you can think of something more romantic."

"Nope. For the rest of our lives, I'm calling it Bullshit."

"You can't be serious," I said. "What guy would want that? I know you can come up with something better. Something

135

more impressive. Something grander, something—"

"Noble?"

Sitting here on the airplane, remembering how outraged I was that afternoon when she not only pissed on my picnic, but named my dick Bullshit—I find myself unable to stop smiling. I fast-forward my time-saved memory an hour, and find us tying the horses to the rail outside the barn, after our very unsatisfying picnic.

"Got everything?" I said, ready to head for the car.

Rachel looked around a moment, then said, "Follow me."

She led me from the far end of the barn to the tack room, next to the wash bays. She opened the door and entered the tiny tack room, and pulled me in behind her. It was dark, and musty, and the air was redolent of moldy old leather. The floor was littered with sawdust and caked mud. Rachel closed the door, locking us inside.

"We've got three minutes, Kevin," she said, "So make them count."

"Why three?" I'd said.

"I just saw a car turning onto the farm road."

"Just so we're clear—"

"Fuck me," she said. "Right here and now. Or never get another chance."

I spun her around, pulled her jeans and panties to her knees, bent her over an elevated saddle, and accomplished all I could in the allotted time. About halfway into it, Rachel said, "Gosh, if only mommy could see me now!"

Her comment gave me the briefest pause, but I quickly put it out of my mind when she shouted "*Harder!*" I obliged her, and abruptly she said, "Time's up."

"What?"

"That's it. Time's up."

"But—"

She reached behind her and pushed me out. Then she turned to face me, got on her knees, and said, "Close your eyes, Kevin, because this is something you're never going to forget."

I did as she said, closed my eyes, and within seconds I was on fire.

"What the *hell?*"

She'd put horse liniment on Bullshit! My crotch smoldered for hours afterward, which proved her right about our first time being something I'd never forget. On the ride home I said, "Why would you do that to me?"

"To make you like me."

"That doesn't make sense."

"If you still want to see me after today, it proves you like me."

"Can you explain the concept a little clearer?"

"You've been with hundreds of women, right?"

"I don't keep count," I said.

"Whatever, stud guy. But you've had plenty."

"So?"

"So you probably did some of them because they were easy, and some you probably cared about enough to create a romantic scene, like you did for me today."

"So?"

"So I bet each woman played along, said and did all the things she was supposed to, and when it was over, you were proud of your conquest. But then you stopped to wonder if she was really as special as you'd thought. And maybe you dumped her, or maybe you stayed with her until the next pretty face came along, and then that one became your challenge."

"What are you trying to say?"

"I took you off your game, hot shot, and out of your routine. I didn't do it to prove I'm special, I did it because I *am* special. And now, instead of wondering if you want to see me again, you're going to realize you *have* to see me again."

"Why's that?"

"Because you're a sick puppy, and what you crave isn't the sex, but the unexpected."

"What are you *talking* about?"

"The minute you can predict a woman's behavior, you get bored. You hit the jackpot with me, because even *I* don't know what I'm going to do or say next."

I chewed on that for awhile, and then asked what she meant back in the tack room when she'd said, "If only mommy could see me now!"

She said, "Mommy died right after daddy, when I was a kid. She didn't have to die, but that's what junkies do, even when they've got a kid to raise. So there I was today, cheating on my husband, bent over a filthy saddle, getting pounded from behind in a barn, like a mare in heat. Don't you suppose mommy would be proud of me?"

Back on the plane now, in real time, I suddenly realize what I'd been missing. There's something I have to do.

I pick up the handset and tell the pilot to land in Atlanta. Then I call Jarvis, and tell him I need his car. When we land, Jarvis is already there. I ask him to wait on the plane with Callie until I return.

33.

FORTY-FIVE MINUTES later I'm in a nice area of Atlanta. It could be any major city, but it happens to be Atlanta. It's well past any normal person's bedtime, so I don't expect Sherry Cherry to be awake. And if she *is* awake, I don't expect her to be sober.

For this reason, instead of calling her on the phone, I break into her house.

Sherry's married name was Birdsong. Personally, I think Birdsong is a great name. But Sherry never liked it. Said it had no pizzazz. So when her husband died shortly after their wedding, she went back to using her maiden name.

Now I'm in the living room and, as I suspected, Sherry Cherry is lying on the couch, strung out on drugs. The only reason she has a house at all is that I bought one and allow her to live here, rent-free.

I park myself in the love seat that faces the couch. The coffee table between us is littered with empty beer bottles, a weed pipe, syringes, zip-lock bags of coke, and assorted drug paraphernalia. Sherry is wearing boxers, white with red hearts, and an oversized man's dress shirt that also happens to be white, except for the stains. The odor of old booze and weed hit me the moment I entered, but now all I can smell is Sherry's urine. At some point in the day or evening she must have pissed herself enthusiastically. Judging from the stain in her boxers and on the couch, it didn't appear to be a recent accident.

I tried to get Sherry into rehab once, but she was too far gone. She checked herself out within an hour after I left. Thinking about Rachel on the jet awhile ago, remembering what she'd said that day in Kentucky after our first time, about how her mother had died because "that's what junkies do," my thoughts turned to Sherry Cherry. I can't save Rachel tonight, and the fact that Lou can't turn up a single piece of information regarding Rachel's whereabouts forces me to consider the possibility I might never see her again.

So I may or may not be able to save the woman I love.

But I can certainly try to save this junkie.

Sherry Cherry is only forty-six. Though she's lived a hard life, she's well put together. Even so, I'm not the least bit aroused when I carry her to her bed, strip her, and give her a sponge bath. She's a nasty mess, and there's nothing sensual about the experience. When I finally get her scrubbed, I dress her in a clean pair of panties, sweatpants, a cotton tee, and light jacket. Then I pack a small bag of clothes and toiletries she won't be able to access anytime soon. I put her over my shoulder, carry her to the car, pour her into the passenger seat, and drive to the runway where I'd been dropped off less than two hours ago.

"Who's this?" Callie says.

"Friend of the family."

"You forgot to brush her teeth."

"You're right."

"If we keep this up," she says, "they're going to run out of beds at Sensory."

"Actually, this one gets a padded room."

Callie yawns. "Can we go now?"

"Yes. After I make a quick call from Jarvis's car."

34.

MY OLD FRIEND Doc Howard is a wealthy man, but not so wealthy he can afford to turn down the opportunity to make a quick hundred million dollars.

"Are we on a secure line?" Doc Howard says.

"Yes. On my side, for certain," I say.

"Mine as well. I have an independent group run a check each week."

"How did you find them?"

"They're ex-CIA. They hate this new bunch I work for at Sensory."

"How do you know these old guys aren't monitoring your line?"

"They could care less what's on my plate. They need quiet doctoring, and I need quiet phone privileges."

I don't need to wonder why Doc Howard needs privacy apart from the things he does for Sensory Resources. After all, he just told me he had some information that was worth a hundred million dollars. I'm sitting in Jarvis's car on the tarmac at the government's restricted airstrip near Atlanta. Callie and the others are on board the jet, waiting for me. I had called Doc Howard to ask about the sudden, intense pain I experienced at the park on Friday night while carrying Frankie the snake, and again a few hours ago in Jane's bedroom. I also wanted to make arrangements at Sensory for our new guests.

But I hadn't gotten either comment out of my mouth before Doc Howard said, "I'm glad you resurfaced. And with all this *money*!"

"I don't know what you're talking about," I say.

"I had an interesting visit with Sam Case today," he says. "By the way, Sam hates you."

"He was probably just angry about the snakebite."

"That too, but he also mentioned you recently put him out of business, stole his wife, and netted about three billion dollars."

"Sam's been known to exaggerate," I say.

"Nevertheless, I'm sure you can spare a hundred million."

"First, let me tell you what I need tonight," I say. "Wait. Are you trying to blackmail me?"

"I'm not insane, Donovan."

"Then what do you mean?"

"If I tried to blackmail you, I'd be dead within minutes. This is completely different. I have information to sell. It's up to you if you don't want to utilize it."

"I'm intrigued," I say, wondering what on earth he could know that would be worth a hundred million dollars to me.

"So what do you need tonight?" he says.

"Callie Carpenter and I are bringing you three more guests. I'd like you to strap Jane and Bernard Asprin to hospital beds, and keep them generally sedated until I have a better use for them."

"And the third guest?"

"We'll call her Paula Asprin," I say. "I want her in a padded cell. She's a junkie. I want to get her clean, and I don't care what it takes. Push her as hard as you need to, without killing her."

"I'm not an expert at drug rehabilitation," he says.

"Then hire someone who is. I'll foot the tab."

"And a high tab it will be," he says.

"I want you to meet us tonight," I say, "and after the others are put to bed, I need you to personally draw three vials of blood from Paula. I want you to personally analyze each of them separately, and privately, and only you and I will know about either the blood work or the results."

"I can do that," he says. "Anything else?"

"I don't want Lou to know about Paula," I say.

"No problem."

"How can you keep this information from Lou? I don't work there anymore."

"Actually, you do. Your office is still here, your sleeping cell, and have you noticed? We're still doing your bidding."

"I *have* noticed. But I thought all this went through Lou."

"It *has* been going through Lou up to now. But according to Darwin, you're still Lou's boss. And as you know, Darwin rules."

That he does. In all the years I've worked for the government, from the Army to the CIA to Homeland Security—I've never encountered a person who wielded the type and degree of power Darwin does. Need a jet? Darwin can get you an aircraft carrier full of them. Want to mess around with a secret weapon? A prototype that's never been used in the field? Call Darwin, and it'll be on your front porch in an hour. Need a mess cleaned up? Like twelve civilians were accidentally killed because we blew up the wrong building? Darwin makes a few calls, bam! No investigation.

"And what did Darwin tell the fine folks at Sensory?" I ask.

"About?"

"About me?"

"He said you were taking a break, but if you ever need something, we're to do it without asking questions."

"What if I ask you to do something that hurts them?"

He chuckles. "Which brings us to the hundred million dollar question."

"Okay," I say. "Shoot."

"It can wait till you get here," he says.

"I remain intrigued," I say.

After ending the call I enter the jet, thank Jarvis for the use of his car, and remind him to stay close to Roger Asprin's daughter, Ellen. After he drives away, our jet takes off.

35.

THE ASPRINS HAVE been situated. Callie's gone to bed. Doc Howard and I are with Sherry Cherry, in a windowless examination room. He's drawing blood from her arm. When we're done, she'll be put in a room with padded walls and flooring.

"What kind of information is worth a hundred million dollars?" I say.

"The chip."

"What chip?"

"This is a little awkward for me."

"Give it your best shot."

"Okay. You remember when you were my patient here at Sensory?"

"Of course. They made you give me a new face."

"They also made me put a chip in your brain that can be accessed by satellite."

"What? You're shitting me!"

"It's not the sort of thing I would joke about," Doc Howard says.

"Can you prove it?"

"I don't have to. You can get a CAT scan from anyplace you choose. You'll see it."

"So what does this mean? They can find me wherever I go?"

Doc Howard removes the needle from Sherry's arm and holds a cotton tab to it for twenty seconds. Then he tapes the tab in place and wraps the tape around her arm to keep it tight.

"I assume you want these results ASAP?" he says.

"Yes. And no other eyes get to see it."

"No problem."

"How many hours will it take?"

"Not hours. Days."

"What? How many?"

"Three. And trust me, that's a blisteringly fast turnaround."

I had to trust him. What do I know about analyzing blood?

"Not to stray from the subject, Doc, but about this chip in my head. They want to know where I am at all times?"

"No. This particular chip is programmed to heat when activated."

I grab his throat with my thumb and index finger. If I squeeze a little harder, he dies. Doc Howard's eyes are bugging out.

"Is this the cause of the headaches I've been experiencing? Did you do that to me?"

He tries to respond, but can't. I release him.

"Jesus, Creed. That happened in less than an eye blink!"

"Try to remember that, next time you fuck with me."

Doc Howard rubs his throat. "Now I know how the mouse feels when the snake strikes."

"You haven't answered my question."

"Yes, I'm responsible. The first time was a test. The second was to confirm."

"Test and confirm what?"

"If I had the right information, and if it worked."

"So you're saying what, they can torture me? How hot will

147

this chip get when they flip the switch?"

"I'll paint you a picture. Have you ever shot a guy and the bullet remained in the body?"

"For the sake of argument, let's assume I have."

"In such a case, the bullet is red hot. Molten-fire hot. So hot it boils the surrounding tissue until the blood itself cools the bullet."

I'm pretty good with pain. If he's talking about the pain a boiling bullet would make in my brain, I can probably handle that. Have, in fact, handled it twice. And the second time was a little easier.

But then Doc Howard says, "The chip I installed is ten times worse. They flip the switch, you're dead within a minute."

"From heat?"

"With every passing second, the chip gets hotter. It will take less than a minute to liquefy your brain."

"Well, how nice of you to put that in my head! Were you ever going to tell me?"

"It's Darwin's news to tell," he says.

"The way I see it, you've given me the information, but I haven't paid you yet."

"True."

"So what's the hundred million dollars for?"

"Ask me if I can remove the chip from your brain."

"Can you?"

"No. And no one else on earth can, either, without killing you. Even if I *could* remove it, Darwin would know."

"I wonder why he's kept it a secret from me," I say.

"I don't know. What I *do* know is they've got a huge amount of time and money invested in you. But they fear you. Darwin probably considers this the ultimate insurance policy."

I can certainly understand it in those terms. I've already got an enormous amount of money on deposit that's generating a hundred million dollar a year income for Darwin. He knows if something happens to me, the monthly flow of money stops. So Darwin should think twice before flipping the switch. On the other hand, Darwin's got plenty of money, so maybe it wouldn't be such a hard decision for him. Then again, why kill the golden goose? My best guess, I'm probably safe from Darwin. But I don't like the idea my brain could liquefy at any given moment.

"Is Darwin the only one who can flip the switch?"

"I honestly don't know," he says.

"How vulnerable am I?"

"They can only kill you via satellite, so if you're living, say, forty feet below the earth, you'd probably be safe."

"Good to know."

"You've had it in there more than a year," he says.

"So?"

"You've lasted this long, you're probably safe."

"Unless the wrong person gets a hold of the switch," I say.

"It's not like an actual switch," he says. "There's a code."

"Who created it?"

"I'm not sure. But I installed the device."

"Ah," I say.

So Doc Howard knows the code. I wonder if I should simply beat it out of him and save the money. But then I remind myself that Doc Howard's a brilliant man. The kind who would have anticipated my first instinct, and have a countermeasure prepared.

Doc Howard says, "I can reprogram the code so that it can't be activated."

"So I'd be paying you to change the code."

"That's right."

"And Darwin will never know."

"Unless he's watching me while I type it in."

"Which is unlikely."

"Here's the best part: if we do this, you'll be able to tell if he ever *does* punch in his code."

"Very valuable piece of information," I say.

"You can see why, right?"

"Of course. Darwin will think I'm dead, and I'll know he tried to kill me."

"Exactly."

"But what prevents you from resetting the code after I pay you?"

"When I verify you've wired the money to my offshore account, I'll show you how to set the code. We'll set a new one together. After that, you can change it whenever you wish."

"Burglar alarms use codes," I say.

He frowns. "They do. What's your point?"

"You can assign me a personal code that will get me in your house without setting off the alarm. And each of your family members can have a different code."

"So?"

"So, what if there's more than one code?"

"I doubt there's more than one access code," he says, "because Darwin would want sole control over your demise. But for the sake of argument, let's assume there's more than one. It doesn't matter, because before you and I can change the code, we have to disable the chip. When that happens, the previous codes are wiped out. It's like pressing the factory reset button on your cell phone."

"What keeps you or Darwin from disabling the chip next week and resetting the code?"

"Well, you've got me there," Doc Howard says. "I'm positive the only way to disable the chip is to have the current code. But I can't prove it. Still, you'll know if someone has done that to you, because when the chip is disabled, it buzzes. It will be very uncomfortable. If you ever feel the buzz, you'll know someone has disabled the chip. When the buzzing stops, you'll know they've set up a new code."

"At which time I can deactivate the chip again?"

"Precisely."

"Is there a way to prove you're giving me the right code?"

"How many brain-burning incidents have you experienced?"

"How many do you *think* I've had?"

"I'm hoping you've had two. The first was Darwin's code, which I attempted to access. The second was mine. The third was Darwin's again, and if I'm right, that one shouldn't have worked."

"So you've proven it to your satisfaction," I say. "Can you prove it to mine?"

He smiles and gestures to the chair by the bed. "Have a seat."

"I'd rather stand."

"Please," he says. "I'm afraid when the pain starts, you might lash out at me, and if that happens, I might not be able to override the sequence in time. My intention is to have you experience as little pain as possible, while proving the lethal nature of the chip."

I frown, then take a seat. "How long are you going to let it run?"

"You won't be able to stand more than two seconds."

"How long could you run it before there's permanent brain damage?"

"I don't know. Maybe ten seconds."

"Run it for nine," I say.

"Donovan. You don't understand. This is not some Army test weapon that's been used on an actual human being. I could be wrong about the ten seconds."

"Doc, look at me." He does. "You expect me to fork over a hundred million dollars based on two seconds' worth of pain?"

"Two seconds should be more than sufficient. And anyway, I'm trying to protect my investment. If your brain turns to mush, you won't be able to wire the money."

"Give me nine seconds. I want my money's worth."

Doc Howard sighs. "Very well." He takes what looks like a fancy wristwatch from his pants pocket, studies it a moment, then presses a button. The face opens up, and he says, "You're going to feel a slight burning sensation."

"Funny."

He taps the device four times and I feel a bomb go off in my head. The pain is excruciating. No, it's worse than that. It feels like...no. There are no words to express it. Example. Example. Example. Okay. If you lay me down on the floor, and take the largest drill you can find, say an inch in diameter, and you drill a one-inch hole in the center of my forehead until you've created a deep cavity, then jam a funnel into it, and pour enough molten lava to fill the cavity, then take a hammer, and pound the lava till it's cooled. Then heat two ice picks until they're as hot as branding irons, and use the hammer to pound the red-hot ice picks into each of my eyes until they've gone all the way to the hilt—do all that, and you might have an inkling what the first second feels like.

The next eight are much worse.

When I come to, Doc Howard and I look at each other a

minute. Then he says, "I can't imagine how you endured that."

I clear my throat, try to speak. Nothing comes out. I swallow a couple of times. Then say, "Is that all you got?"

He laughs. "You're one of a kind, Donovan."

"As you are," I say.

"So what do you think about my offer? Is a hundred million a fair price?"

"It was a rough ride," I admit. "But the pain was manageable. A few more seconds and I wouldn't have felt anything anyway, so it's not the worst way I can think of to die. But what I can't abide is letting Darwin kill me any time it suits him, from anywhere in the world. If you can help me prevent that, then your offer is a bargain."

"No hard feelings?" he says.

"You're screwing Darwin, not me. And if he finds out you reset his code—"

"If he finds out, you'll know it, and I'll trust you to deal with it," Doc Howard says.

"You better hope I do."

"I'm betting my life on you."

In a strange way, I'm flattered. I mean, sure, he's gaining a hundred million dollars. But he also thinks I can handle Darwin, and all of Darwin's resources, which makes me feel like the owner of Seabiscuit, going against War Admiral, knowing the fans have bet their life's savings on the underdog.

"Doc, I'm not happy you put the chip in my brain, but I understand why you did it. I know you're feathering your nest at my expense, but the truth is, I'm only giving you a small portion of the money I stole from someone else. So how can I blame you? We're probably both getting tired of doing some of the things we've done. But I still need you to help me save Rachel, and I know there'll be a hundred things I'll need from you in the future. So I'd like to consider this payment a cost of doing business with you.

"Honestly?"

I shrug. "All honesty is contextual. But if you do everything I ask of you with regard to these Asprin people, especially the one we're calling Paula, and you keep these results between the two of us, I'll wire the money to your account."

36.

IT'S 9:00 P.M., and the only sleep I've logged since Sam's "reveal" occurred at altitude as I criss-crossed the continent. Fourteen hours have passed since Doc Howard burned my brain for nine full seconds, and I'm still feeling the after-effects.

Callie and I are standing in the eighth-floor hallway of the Lucian-Jevere Hotel and Conference Center in Chicago. After checking for cameras, I stand out of view while Callie knocks on the door of Roger Asprin's suite. It's late, and Chicago's a dangerous place, but Callie is Callie, and of course, Roger opens the door. She punches his throat hard enough to keep him from crying out, then pushes him back into his room as she enters. I slip in behind them and lock the door.

It's just like old times. Roger can't scream because I've injected his vocal chords with an anesthetic. I've got a tracheal tube kit open and ready to use in the event his neck swells enough to impair his oxygen supply.

"I know you can't speak," I say, "but you can hear and feel things."

He shakes his head as if to indicate I'm wrong. Callie kicks him in the nuts and his eyes roll up in his head. He'd kick us if he could, but I've got his legs tied to either side of the desk chair I've placed in the center of his bedroom. Unlike Hector, Roger's wearing underwear. He also sports a T-shirt, though not for long. I rip it off.

"You know what really hurts?" I say.

Then I show him.

Ten minutes later, tears are streaming from Roger's bloodshot eyes. I say, "Roger, I know you're in pain, probably the worst you've ever had to endure. But I promise you, everything I've done so far will seem like a day at the spa compared to what I *will* do, if you refuse to cooperate."

I look at Callie. "You hungry?"

"I could eat a bite," she says.

"Roger, we're going to order room service. By the time we're done, you'll be able to whisper some answers."

I'm not wild about the in-room dining options on the menu, but the baked penne arrabiatta looks okay. Callie wants the Caesar salad, until I explain it includes white anchovies and a boiled egg.

"I don't like hairy fish," she says, "and boiled eggs do not belong in a Caesar salad."

"I agree about the egg," I say, "but I think you'll like the anchovies."

"Why's that?"

"They're marinated in white vinegar instead of salt-cured and packed in oil, like regular anchovies. Of course, fresh are best, but where are you going to find those?"

"They can keep their albino anchovies," she says. "Their little pink eyes give me the creeps."

I wonder if I should explain these aren't albino anchovies, then realize, who gives a shit? She doesn't want the salad.

"How about the braised pork shank and black forest mushroom risotto?" I say.

"Lips that touch pork shank shall never touch mine," Callie says.

I hand her the menu. She reads it, frowning, until she suddenly smiles.

"What have you found?" I ask.

"The kids' menu."

"Chicken fingers? Pizza?"

"Nope. Strawberries and Rice Krispies. Call it in, Coleman."

"Coleman?"

"From *Trading Places*."

"Ah. Winthorpe's butler."

After the room-service guy leaves, I open the door so we can keep an eye on Roger.

We enjoy our food in silence. When we're finished, Callie says, "What sort of name is Asprin?"

"Nordic."

"You are so full of shit."

I shrug. "Busted."

From the next room, Roger makes a hissing sound. His mouth is moving up and down like a fresh-caught bass out of water.

"Is that our cue?" Callie says.

"It is."

37.

"*WHO ARE YOU? What do you want? Why are you doing this to me?*" Roger Asprin whispers.

"I'm going to answer your questions in the order you asked them," I say. "Who are we? I'm Donovan Creed, and this is Callie Carpenter. What do we want? Rachel Case."

Roger's eyes grow wide. He starts to speak. I hold up my hand to stop him. "Why are we doing this to you? Because you're the only person in the world who can help us get Rachel back. But the real question you should be asking is this: what are we willing to do in order to get what we want? Because here's the thing, Roger: we've got your wife. Callie, show him the video feed."

Callie holds her cell phone where Roger can see Jane in the hospital bed at Sensory.

"You see how she's fighting against the straps? She's really angry, Roger. But soon she's going to be very frightened, instead. You can save her, or you can watch her die a slow, painful death."

"You don't understand," Roger whispers. "We're saving mankind."

"You don't kidnap and kill people to save mankind," I say. "You killed Rachel's doctor. You tried to kill her caretaker. You want to save the world? Fine. Ask?"

"Ask?"

"Yeah, that's right, asshole. You could've asked Rachel to help you."

Roger swallows, clears his throat. His voice is starting to come back, but it's hoarse.

"Cough a couple of times," I say. "That should help."

He does. "There are—" his voice cracks.

I hold up my hand again. "Take a minute. We can't understand what you're saying."

He coughs a couple more times. Then says, "There are people in the world who would use her as a weapon. They could literally wipe out a significant percentage of the earth's population."

"Our government could do the same."

"No. We're saving the world. You have no idea. This is the breakthrough we've sought for more than 70 years."

"Is curing the Spanish flu worth dying for?"

"Yes, of course."

"Is it worth watching your wife tortured to death?"

"If that's your plan, I'd rather you kill me first. But yes, it's worth Jane's suffering. Except that it's pointless."

"I'm listening," I say.

"There's nothing I can do to help you, even if I wanted to."

"Which you don't."

"Of course not."

Callie and I exchange a glance. She accesses Bernard's live feed, then positions it where Roger can see.

"Your son, Bernard," I say.

"What's happened to his *leg*?" Roger yells.

"We cut it off. Shall we lop off one of his arms while you watch?"

Roger starts to cry.

"Callie, show him the Atlanta feed."

She punches some keys on her cell phone. When the video comes up, she holds it in front of Roger's face.

"That's your daughter Ellen's house. Your son-in-law's out of town on business. Ellen's taking a bath right now, listening to music. Your granddaughter, Bug, is upstairs in her crib, sleeping soundly. A simple phone call changes all that."

"Kill them all," Roger says. "And kill me, too."

"You're not serious," I say.

"I've devoted my entire life to finding a cure," he says, through his tears. "You can torture, maim, and kill every person I hold dear. But I wouldn't help you rescue Rachel Case even if I could. Because no matter what you do to me, or those I love, the greater good demands that a cure be made available to mankind. You have no idea what this disease will do when it resurfaces."

"I like you, Roger, I really do. It's dedicated people like you that help keep us safe. You make the world a better place. But make no mistake, I *am* going to kill you if I don't get Rachel back. After I force you to watch your loved ones die. Because Rachel doesn't deserve this. And neither do her unborn children."

"How do you know about that?"

"Rachel's husband is a genius. I told him about Rachel's blood test, and about how your people killed her doctor, and within hours he came up with the answer."

"Mr. Creed," Roger said.

"Yes?"

"Sam Case works for us."

38.

I CAN'T GET my cell phone open fast enough.

"Lou! Where's Sam?"

"Bluemont, Virginia."

"*What?* Why?"

"You said to take him where he wanted to go."

"*Fuck!*"

"What's wrong?"

"Hold on."

I give Roger Asprin my most menacing look. "Where's Rachel? Tell me and I'll spare one of your family members. You have my word."

"I—I can't."

"Callie, tell Jarvis to kill Ellen. Drown her in her tub."

"No!" Roger cries.

"And tell Jarvis I want a video feed. Have him hold her under with one hand and video her with the other. I want Roger to see what he's forced us to do."

Callie punches a button on her speed dial.

"After he kills Ellen, tell him to go upstairs and stand outside Bug's room and wait for further instructions."

To Roger I say, "This is your last chance. You don't even have to name the place they're holding Rachel, because I already know. All you have to do is verify it. She's at Mount Weather, isn't she?"

Callie says, "Jarvis? It's showtime."

Roger says, "Wait!"

I hold up my hand.

Callie says, "Just a minute. Mr. Creed might grant a stay of execution."

Roger says, "She's in the hospital at Mount Weather."

"Callie," I say, "Tell Jarvis to stand down."

"Sorry, Jarvis," she says. "You're going to have to wait awhile." She ends the call.

To Roger I say, "Does Sam have access?"

"Access?"

"Clearance. Whatever you call it."

"I'm not sure I—"

I slap his face. "Is Sam able to gain entry into Mount Weather?"

"Yes, of course."

To Lou I say, "What do you know about the facility at Mount Weather?"

"No more than you, I expect," he says.

"Ever been inside?"

"No. You?"

"No."

We're silent awhile, realizing what we're up against. Finally Lou says, "We're screwed."

"Not yet," I say.

39.

HERE'S WHAT I know about the facility at Mount Weather: it's more than a hundred years old. There's an underground bunker the size of a small city, built to withstand repeated direct strikes from nuclear weapons. It's where the top government officials were taken by helicopter after the 9/11 attacks, because their lives are so much more valuable than those of us who elected them. I also know this: there has never been a security breach at Mount Weather.

Lou calls me back after doing a quick computer search and adds the following details: "There's an above-ground section of more than 400 acres, called Area A. The underground bunker, Area B, is more than 600,000 square feet in size, and contains a hospital, crematorium, dining and recreational facilities, self-contained power plants, and is equipped to broadcast TV and radio."

I was suddenly worried that Sam might be able to determine how close Sensory Resources is to Mount Weather.

"What route did you take to get him there?" I ask. "You didn't just drive him straight to Bluemont, did you?"

"Of course not. We blindfolded him, sedated him, flew him to Atlanta, stopped, woke him up, drove him to Macon, sedated him again, then flew him back to Sensory, and drove him to Bluemont, still blindfolded."

"What about his cell phone?" I had removed the battery

because I didn't want him using his GPS system to determine where he was. But he could always get another battery.

"We destroyed the cell phone. But Sam's a bright guy. He could figure out a way to contact people without it."

"True. But he wouldn't be able to tell where he's been."

"Well, at least our location appears to be safe."

We're both trying to keep from stating the obvious. That Sam is in the bunker with Rachel, and for now, there's nothing we can do about it.

"Thanks, Lou. You did everything right. But we both know he's in there with her."

"Do you have a plan to get her out?"

"I do."

"How can I help?"

"For now, sit tight."

To Roger I say, "When did Sam start working with you?"

"Let my family go, and I'll tell you everything I know."

"Why the sudden change of heart?"

"Because killing my family won't help you get what you want. And when I tell you everything I know, you'll see that I can't help you, either."

"I'll spare Bug if you tell me what you know about Sam. Or I can kill Ellen while you think about it."

"I have your word about sparing my granddaughter?"

"You do. Unless I catch you in a lie, in which case she'll be the first to go."

"I'll tell the truth, as I know it."

"Go ahead, then."

"I don't know when these events first occurred," Roger says, "but Sam made his deal after the first kidnapping."

"What kidnapping are you talking about? Dr. D'Angelo?"

"Is that Rachel's doctor?"

"He *was* her doctor."

"Well, you say he's been killed, but I don't know anything about that." He takes a breath, fighting to make his voice clear. Then says, "All I've heard is that Rachel Case went to a doctor and gave blood for the first time in her life. When our computers generated a match, the Department of Health contacted whoever they contact for such matters of national security, and they went to Rachel's home to extract her."

"That's ancient history. What's all this about the first kidnapping?"

"When Rachel filled out the forms at the doctor's office, she used her old address, from when she lived with Sam. That's where the security team went to find her, but of course, she was living somewhere else. Sam agreed to cooperate, on the condition we put him in the loop. When he learned why we wanted her, and where we planned to keep her, he gave the team her new address, and even provided a key to her apartment."

His comment about the key hits me hard. If Roger's telling the truth, Rachel's been in contact with Sam, and gave him a key. I think about that a moment. No. She wouldn't give him a key. Like Lou said, Sam's a clever guy. He found a way to get a copy of Rachel's house key. I don't know how, but I'm certain she didn't give him a key.

"Did he go with the team to kidnap Rachel last Monday?"

"I don't know. I *do* know that Sam's only condition for helping us was that he be allowed to live in Area B as long as Rachel was there. We agreed, because he's her husband, and because he's brilliant. He plans to work full-time to help us develop a synthetic gene, based on Rachel's blood cells. Of course, being her husband, it makes sense that he live there, because he and Rachel can raise their children together."

"Rachel is an unwilling participant in this scheme."

Roger Asprin smiles wearily. "Aren't we all?"

"So Sam's plan is to buddy up to her, and manipulate her into getting back with him. Meanwhile, he gets to work on the synthetic gene that can cure the Spanish flu, at which point he'll be a hero. You guys will release them both, and he will have saved her and their children."

"You think he can do all that?" Roger says.

"I don't give a shit. I want her back. And I'm willing to kill your family to get her."

"How will killing my family bring Rachel back?"

"It won't. But using them as a bargaining chip might. I'll spare your family, and your life as well, if you tell the scientists you were wrong about Rachel's blood."

"But I wasn't wrong."

"I understand that. But if you tell them you made a mistake, they'll have no reason to hold her there. Especially if it means keeping the heat off the government."

"What heat?"

"Ever hear of WikiLeaks?"

"Of course."

"They're one of more than a hundred international sources I plan to use to announce what's happening in Area B with Rachel, and how you plan to harvest her eggs and keep her children hostages forever."

"Not forever. Just until we can develop a synthetic form of the gene."

"How long will that take?"

"Ten years, give or take."

"That's unacceptable."

"Is this your plan?" Roger says.

"It is."

"It won't work. The government will discredit your announcement as so much nonsense. They'll call it the latest conspiracy theory. In the absence of any hard evidence to back up your story, your information sources will quickly pull your comments, to avoid looking foolish. Not only that, but the idea of a human conduit to the Spanish flu virus is so unimaginable, I doubt the respected news stations will even broadcast your story."

"I don't buy that, and when it comes down to watching us put a knife to your children's throats, I think you'll choose to let your family live. All you have to do to save them is tell your people that Rachel's blood cells don't match after all."

"That's the other part of your plan that won't work."

"Why not?"

"You're too late," Roger says.

"What do you mean?"

"I already gave them the go-ahead, based on the preliminary tests. That's why we allowed Sam to enter the facility yesterday. The project has been given a green light. As a bonus, Rachel has already given us an egg to test."

Crestfallen, I look at Callie for support.

"I'm sorry, Donovan," she says. "But that sounds like game, set and match. We can still kill his kids, though."

"Wait here," I say.

I leave the room, take the elevator to the parking garage, and get my duffel bag from the trunk of my rental car. When I get back to Roger's room, I open the case and remove a metal cuff. After attaching it to Roger's left ankle, I say, "You're going to wear this until I personally remove it. In the meantime, you're going to continue hosting the conference, and I'm going to be fifteen feet away from you, day and night, until it's over. In addition, you'll have no use of your cell phone, and I'll be in your room, to monitor your calls."

"You can't just show up at this conference. It's by invitation only. The world's greatest scientists are there. Government officials. Ministers of Health from around the world—"

"And me."

"How can I possibly explain your presence?"

"Tell them I'm your government-appointed bodyguard."

He thinks about it. Then says, "What about my family?"

"I'll hang onto them awhile longer."

"You've cut off my son's leg. How do I know he's receiving proper treatment?"

"You'll have to trust us on that."

"What about the private meetings I have to attend? The one-on-ones? You can't be privy to those exchanges."

"I can and I will. You'll have to think up a way to explain my presence."

He sighs. "What's the ankle band for?"

"It contains an explosive device. If you so much as hint that something's amiss, I'll detonate the cuff. When I do, it'll take out everything in a twelve-foot radius."

"What do you hope to achieve by doing this?"

"I intend to rescue Rachel."

"But I've already explained. That's impossible."

"Plan A might be impossible. But I've got a Plan B."

40.

"WHAT'S PLAN B?" Callie asks. We're sitting in the parlor. Close enough to see Roger lying on the floor in the bedroom, far enough to keep from being heard.

"Plan B is a shot in the dark. A last-second buzzer-beater."

"Care to be more specific?"

"You remember the crack whore I put on the jet in Atlanta? The one I put in a padded cell?"

"Of course."

"That's Rachel's mother."

"What? I thought her mother was deceased."

"Everyone thinks that. But I lived in Rachel's attic for nearly two years, watching her every move. I went through all her papers. I listened as she talked in her sleep on the nights I drugged her. I came to realize Rachel's mother was dead to her, but very much alive. If you can call it living. I spent months searching for her, and finally found her. I sat with her until she was coherent, spoke to her about her daughter, and put her in rehab, hoping to reunite them."

"What happened?"

"She relapsed the same day. But I bought a house she could live in, until I decided to make another run at cleaning her up. I just haven't gotten around to doing it till now."

"If Rachel suspected her mother was alive, why didn't you tell her you'd found her?"

"Rachel hates her mother for abandoning her. As far as she's concerned, her mother's dead. She's listed both her parents as deceased on all paperwork she's filled out as an adult. Not only that, but she's told everyone who's asked, that her mother killed herself with drugs. If I'd told Rachel I found her mother, but she's back on smack, it wouldn't have been much of a reunion."

Callie and I are quiet a minute. Then she says, "I don't understand how getting Rachel's mother sober will help you save Rachel."

"It won't. Unless her blood contains the gene."

Callie smiles. "Has she never given blood either?"

"Obviously not. Or if she did, it wasn't picked up by the government's computers."

"Or maybe she wasn't a match."

"Also possible," I say.

Callie frowns. "If Plan B fails, what's left?"

"I'll have to offer them something so politically valuable, they'll be willing to walk away from a cure for the Spanish flu."

"What could possibly be that valuable to them?"

"I don't know. What if I bring them Bin Laden?"

"Excuse me?"

"I know it sounds desperate…"

"Crazy is what it sounds. Tell me you don't know where he's hiding!"

"Of course not. But how hard could it be?"

"Are you shitting me?"

"Look, I haven't discarded Plan B yet."

"How can I help you?" Callie says. "With Plan B, that is."

"I'll handle it from here. I'll have Lou get you back to LA so you can pick up your car."

"I don't mind staying."

"I know, and I appreciate it. But for now, all I can do is wait for Sherry's blood tests to come back."

"Doc Howard?"

"Yup."

"And of course, his computers won't be linked to a different branch of the government."

"Darwin would never allow it."

"Well, I hope it works. If it doesn't, are you still going to kill Roger and his family?"

"What type of hit man would I be if I didn't?"

41.

FOR THE NEXT three days I'm on Roger Asprin like his shadow. The only breaks I take are to check on Nadine, who has been released and is back in Rachel's apartment. At night, in his hotel room, Roger and I talk. He's a decent guy who loves his wife and kids. I feel terrible that his wife is cheating on him, but it's not my place to tell him about it. On the other hand, Roger's being very forthright with me, hoping, I assume, that if we're friends, I'll let his family go. On the third night, I ask, "Tell me how this harvesting works."

Roger looks up from the notes he'd been studying and says, "Rachel's eggs?"

I nod.

"It involves in vitro fertilization. Now that she's given her first egg, they'll administer a series of fertility drugs to stimulate her ovaries to produce a number of eggs at the same time. Removing the eggs from her ovaries will require minor surgery."

"It's unnatural."

"Everything about this science is unnatural," Roger says.

"Who fertilizes the eggs? A sperm donor? Who carries the babies to term? A surrogate?"

"You're not going to like this."

"Say it anyway."

"Since Sam is Rachel's husband, they'll mix his sperm with

her eggs in the hospital's laboratory. If embryos develop, they'll be grown in a lab dish until one or more are placed into the uterus of the surrogate."

"The babies would belong to the surrogate, though," I say.

"Under normal circumstances, they would. But in this case, they'll belong to the government, though I expect Rachel and Sam will be allowed to raise them and keep them, after the synthetic gene is created."

Before I have a chance to comment, my cell phone rings. Doc Howard says, "I'm not sure what we're looking for, but you were right about the blood tests."

"How's that?"

"They show substantial contamination."

"All three?"

"All three."

"Can your fax be traced?"

"No, of course not."

"Then send them to me."

"Where?"

"I don't officially have a room here, so fax them to Roger Asprin." I give him the name and phone number of the hotel. Moments later, Roger's phone rings. I tell the front-desk lady I'm sending Donovan Creed down to pick it up. The first thing I do is check to make sure there's no phone number or point of origin on the pages. Once satisfied, I go back to Roger's room and hand him one of the pages.

"Where did you get this?" he says. There's alarm in his voice. Or maybe it's excitement.

"Is it a match?" I say.

"It's Rachel's blood work," Roger says.

"There are two more," I say, handing him the other results.

"Who gave you these?"

"A new donor."

"This must be a trick of some sort."

"It's no trick," I say. "It's Plan B."

"What's Plan B?"

"These blood tests came from Rachel's mother."

"Rachel's parents are deceased. We checked. And there are no siblings."

"The papers in your hand suggest otherwise. Anyway, I'm willing to exchange her for Rachel."

"What?"

"You need the gene, Rachel's mother has it. I'll trade you the mom for the daughter."

"She'd be willing to do that?"

"Who gives a shit? I can deliver her. That's all you need to know."

Roger shakes his head. "It won't work."

"Why not?"

"Because they'll want both of them. They won't give one up for the other, especially not the daughter for the mother. Her mother is almost certainly too old to produce eggs."

"True."

Roger says, "You must have realized that all along. I mean, surely you didn't think we'd accept such a trade."

"I did and still do."

"It won't work. And now that we know about Rachel's mother, it'll be impossible for you to hide her."

"I don't need to hide her."

"What do you mean?"

"Plan B isn't just about trading Rachel for her mom. It's about keeping her in the USA. You might have Rachel, but if you refuse to trade, I'll sell her mother to the highest bidding enemy. Who knows what type of mutant virus they might be able to produce and unleash on the world."

"You wouldn't do that."

"I would and I will. So here's Plan B: I let you live, let your family live, and trade you Rachel's mom for Rachel. Which means our government, and not our enemies, will have Rachel's mom. In addition, I'll put the lid on the worldwide announcement I'm prepared to make about what's going on at Mount Weather. Now that I have proof of a genetic code, the world will take me seriously."

"You don't understand. We need Rachel's eggs."

"You can keep her long enough to get one more."

"We'll want at least a dozen embryos."

"You've already got one."

"We have an egg, Donovan. Not an embryo."

"I'll personally deliver her eggs to you until you get a dozen embryos. After you let her go. On one condition."

"What's that?"

"You have to keep Sam in Area B for the rest of his life. So he, along with his mother-in-law, can care for his children. I'm sure the children will benefit from having not only their father, but their grandmother as well."

Despite the gravity of the discussion, Roger had to smile. "You'd stick that poor man in a hole with his mother-in-law for the rest of his life? After removing his wife?"

I shrugged. "What do you think?"

42.

IT MAKES SENSE to let Rachel stay underground long enough to produce a few eggs for the scientists. After all, Sherry Cherry will be in no condition to travel for at least a couple of months. I know the government won't want this deal, but Roger will be very persuasive that it's a good one. I'm counting on him to make a passionate argument for the deal, since everyone he loves will die if he doesn't.

43.

SOME PEOPLE MIGHT question what kind of person would kidnap Rachel's mother and force her to live in an underground hole for years and possibly the rest of her life to be a guinea pig for science. The answer is, I'm the type who'd do that, and I'd do it without hesitation. I'm not happy about the idea of Rachel's kids being imprisoned for the next ten years or more, but I don't know them, and apparently they'll be Sam and Rachel's kids, or the government's, so I'll have to deal with it.

44.

IT TAKES EIGHT days before the deal is struck, during which time Sherry Cherry's blood work results are passed around the scientific community like panties in a prison yard. Seven of the days were spent trying to figure out where I'm hiding Sherry, and whether or not they can kill me before I turn her over to some radical enemy group. Roger was right, I'd never do that, but over the years I've developed a reputation with the government that leads them to believe there isn't anything I wouldn't do.

45.

IN THE END, I don't get everything I want, but I do get Rachel back. In six months.

Roger was right about Uncle Sam wanting at least a dozen embryos, and for some reason, they didn't trust me to deliver the balance of them. I agreed to let them harvest all the eggs they can for the next six months, and that should give them enough to work with. In the meantime, I'm certain a genius like Sam could cut the ten-year timetable for creating the synthetic gene to two or three. He'll have the built in motivation of wanting to escape from the hole. Six hundred thousand square feet of living space will seem awfully small after a few years of living with his mother-in-law!

That's the other part I didn't get in the bargain. They refuse to hold Sam against his will for the rest of his life. They also refuse to deny him access to Rachel, which is the part that upsets me the most. But they do allow me to call her once a week, to keep her spirits lifted.

The first time I called she said, "I have no idea who you are." Then she hung up. The next week she said, "I was just kidding." Then she hung up. I can't wait to hear what she says next week when I call. But that's Rachel, ever unpredictable, still keeping me off my game.

46.

I'M NOT THRILLED about what's going on in Area B, but I'm glad to know dedicated scientists like Roger are working day and night to protect the world from the Spanish flu. I hate to wait six months to hold Rachel in my arms, but I know the government will take good care of her. I expect they'll even provide a qualified therapist to work on her mental health.

The six months gives Sherry plenty of time to get better, too. I'm pretty sure Rachel will be upset when she learns I stuck her mother in the hole for however many years she'll have to stay there, but she won't know about it until Sam gets out and tells her. By then, maybe her mother will also be released, and she'll be clean and sober to boot. Rachel might end up having a relationship with her mother after all, in which case I could come out of this whole situation smelling like a rose.

Of course, I had to clear it with Darwin. There's no way I could keep Sherry Cherry's whereabouts a secret without his help. In return, he expects me to go back to work for him full-time, killing suspected terrorists for Uncle Sam. I'm willing to do that, since I miss the excitement. Not to mention it's what I do best.

Now that I've got my deal, the first order of business is to pay off Doc Howard and get the code, so I can protect my brain in case Darwin decides to renege on our deal.

It will all work out.

Roger's happy. He got his family back. He was thrilled to learn that Bernard's leg is still attached to his body. That bed with a hole in it has gotten a lot of use these past few weeks.

Back at Sensory, Doc Howard and I reprogram the chip. Then I reprogram it again, on my own. Then Lou and I meet to discuss Sherry Cherry.

"In a few months not only will Sherry be drug-free for the first time in twenty years, she also gets the opportunity to watch her grandchildren grow up," I say, putting a positive spin on things.

"Lucky Sam," Lou says, chuckling.

"Maybe they'll bond," I say.

The next day I escort Jane and Bernard—still sedated—back to LA. Roger helps me get them in his house, and I leave it to him to come up with an explanation for what's happened to them over the past ten days.

I get a hotel room on the beach in Santa Monica and take two full days to recharge my batteries. Then I order a jet to fly me to New York City for my date with Miranda. On the way there, I call Billy "the Kid" King.

"I'm on my way to New York," I say, cheerfully.

"I'm carrying a gun," he says.

"What kind?"

"Smith & Wesson, .357 Magnum."

"The four-inch?"

"I don't know. Whatever it is."

"Well, I think you've made a good choice," I say.

"Yeah, why's that?"

"Revolvers are simple. They don't jam, so they're reliable. They're small enough to carry, powerful enough to stop a man. Make sure you've got it with you when I see you."

"Why?"

"I can always use another gun in my collection."

There is dead silence on the phone.

"Billy? Are you still on the line?"

In a very small voice, Billy says, "How can I make this stop?"

"I thought you'd welcome the opportunity to see me again. Prove to your friends I was lucky the first time."

"You weren't lucky. I just want to be left alone."

I think about it a minute.

"You really want me out of your life?"

"More than anything."

"Miranda's trying to put herself through school."

"So?"

"If you write her a check to cover her next semester, I'll leave you alone."

"I can't write a check to a hooker! What if she takes it to the police? Isn't that what happened to Jerry Springer? I'd lose my broker's license!"

"You make a good point. Pay her in cash. Fifty grand."

"What? That's insane!"

"No, seriously. Tuition, books, study materials—I don't know how parents do it these days. Student loans, I guess. But Miranda's trying to avoid all that."

"By shaking me down."

"You're the one that punched her, Billy."

"We were being playful. Things got out of hand."

"Right."

We were quiet a moment. Then I said, "So, you want me to pick it up personally?"

"Can we do it another way?"

"You know Guy at the gym? Z's friend?"

"Yeah."

"Put the cash in a duffel and give it to him."

"I don't want the guys in the gym to know about this."

"That makes sense. Tell you what. I'm staying at the Pierre. Put the cash in a box, wrap it like a birthday present, and leave it at the front desk for me."

"How do I know you'll give it to the hooker?"

"Does it really matter?"

"What if you take the money and claim I never brought it?"

"Billy, listen to me. I'm a billionaire. I'd rather break your nose every time I come to town than steal your money. You asked what it would take for me to go away, and I've told you. But there's one caveat."

"What now?"

"You have to promise to stay away from her."

"No problem."

"I'm serious, Billy."

"Me too."

"No running into her, no booking her under an assumed name, no following her around."

"The bitch is nothing but trouble. I never want to see her again."

"In that case, we've got a deal."

"What time should I bring the box?"

"Anytime tomorrow before five p.m. Surprise me."

"You trust the front desk?"

"Billy. It's the Pierre."

"Okay."

47.

MIRANDA RODRIQUEZ LOOKS like a million dollars. Then again, I love watching a gorgeous girl dig into a sixteen-ounce prime strip steak and a side of skillet potatoes and onions.

"Are we really going to see *Jersey Boys* tonight?" she says.

"We are."

"That is so cool!"

Cool. Sometimes, when I forget I'm twice her age, she brings me back to reality with a single word like "cool". She's trying to say the right thing, but "awesome" is what she'd say if I were her age. "Cool" doesn't sound right, coming from her twenty-year-old throat. I catch myself wondering what Rachel would have said, and come up with nothing. Because the fact is, Rachel is exactly what she claimed to be that very first day we had sex: unpredictable.

We're at Del Frisco's in Midtown, and my favorite waiter, Rob, is working hard to make me look good in front of my date. He brings us a couple of pineapple-infused vodka martinis. Miranda takes a sip and swoons.

"Oh…my…God!" she says. "This is to die for!"

She's wearing the low-cut burgundy petal dress I bought her earlier this afternoon. After spending an hour trying to find matching shoes, I talked her into a pair of black ("goes with anything") triple-platform strappy sandals with 5¾-inch heels that make her six feet tall.

"Do your feet hurt yet?" I ask.

"If they start to, I'll deal with it," she says, with a wink.

Normally I wouldn't put a lady in such a pair of shoes. But the way her eyes lit up this afternoon when lifting the display shoe to inspect it, rendered me incapable of saying no.

"There are only so many years you can wear something like that," I say. "May as well enjoy it while you can."

Miranda doesn't know it yet, but there's a comfortable pair of black sandals in the box Billy left for me at the front desk. I opened it earlier, to check the contents, and tossed the shoes in as an afterthought. I'll give her the present after the show, when her feet are killing her. The fifty grand should have a soothing effect as well.

"You're pensive," she says. "Anything wrong? Please say no!"

I smile. "That dress looks fantastic on you."

"Wait till you see how it looks on the floor tonight," she purrs.

I already know how it's going to go. We'll have a great time at the show, we'll go to her place afterward, and she'll be overwhelmed by the cash. She'll say and do all the right things. When we start having sex, she'll pretend I'm a stallion. She'll start whimpering that breath-catching sound Hollywood taught women to identify with orgasm. It'll start with a low moan, and build to a crescendo worthy of a porn star. She'll throw in a few "Oh, God's" and maybe call out my name. I start to say something about all this, and then change my mind.

"I'm sorry," Miranda says. "I didn't hear you."

I had started to say, *If we wind up in bed tonight, will you do me a favor?* And she would have said, *Of course.* And I would have said, *Could you be perfectly quiet while we have sex?* And she would have said, *Of course.* And the fact that she wouldn't have asked me why, or gotten the least bit offended about my asking, is why I decided not to pose the question in the first place. Because each brick of predictability might eventually pile up and make a wall between us.

"Donovan?" she says.

"Sorry. I was going to ask if you wanted me to order a soufflé."

"You're so sweet!" She touches my arm with her hand. "I couldn't possibly. Is that okay?"

"Perfectly."

Rachel thinks she knows me, but there's a lot to be said for predictability. By the time we get to Miranda's place tonight, my body will be screaming for her to relieve the sexual tension that's been building up all afternoon. It's a joy to know that having sex tonight is a foregone conclusion. I'll not only get sex tonight, but it will be whatever type of sex I'm in the mood for. Of course, this is less a function of predictability than it is a feature of paying a hooker for her time.

Wait. That's not a fair characterization. Miranda's a courtesan, not a hooker.

But still.

As a plus, I won't have to worry about falling asleep and possibly getting my throat slit, which is more a function of being with a sane woman than being with Rachel, who I love dearly.

Another excellent feature of being with a courtesan is, whatever I say will be fascinating to her. And damn it, sometimes it's nice to be able to just say anything that's on your mind, knowing the woman you're with is not going to give you a look of disgust, or indignation. In fact, there's nothing I can say to Miranda right now that would make her say, *That's disgusting! I hope you're happy, you just ruined my dinner!*"

Want an example? Check this out:

"Miranda?"

"Yes, honey?"

"Did you know there was a time in history when the entire world ran out of coffins?"

"What? Oh, my God! Really?"

"Yup."

"What happened?"

"Ever hear about the Spanish flu pandemic of 1918?"

"No. Please tell me!"

—See what I mean? I'm with a beautiful girl half my age. I'm enjoying a wonderful dinner, getting ready to see an incredible show. I'm a fascinating conversationalist, and I'm going to get laid tonight by a woman whose mission in life is to be the best fuck I've ever had.

Want another example of how I can say anything to Miranda and not get in trouble? "Honey?" I say.

"Yes?"

"Have I ever told you I'm in love with a girl named Rachel?"

"I don't think so, not that I recall."

"Are you jealous?"

"Who wouldn't be? She's got to be the luckiest woman in the whole world!"

"You think?"

"I do," she says. "But not tonight."

"No?"

"Nope. 'Cause tonight, I'm the luckiest woman in the world!"

I hoist my vodka martini and realize with all this going for me, something's missing.

What's that? You think what's missing at this moment is Rachel?

What're you, nuts?

I lift my chin in Rob's direction, and my overly attentive waiter instantly appears.

"Yes, Mr. Creed?"

"Do you happen to have any single-barrel Kentucky bourbon in this joint?"

Rob smiles. "We do, indeed, sir!"

"Would you be so kind?"

"Absolutely, sir! And would the lady care for some?"

Miranda looks at me. Most women hate bourbon, and I'm sure she's no exception.

"That sounds delightful!" she says.

Rob leaves to fetch our bourbon, and I notice Miranda is squirming slightly.

"Are you okay?" I ask.

She gives me a shy, practiced smile, looks down at her hand. My eyes follow hers. She opens it, revealing the tiniest pair of black panties.

"A present," she says.

"For me?"

"Uh huh."

She smiles again.

"If you put them in your jacket pocket, only you and I will know it's not a handkerchief!"

She kisses her panties and hands them to me. I put them where my pocket square had been, and never bother wondering how many men she's said that to before tonight.

Is she pretending?

Of course.

Do I care?

Of course not. In truth, I'm beginning to question how much of a future I have with Rachel. Her unpredictability has become predictable.

Maybe I'll pretend something too. Maybe I'll pretend the fifty grand is a present from me. Am I capable of doing something that shady, just to enrich my status in her eyes?

Of course I am. But will I?

I haven't decided yet.

Rob brings us a shot of premium bourbon.

Miranda and I share a toast.

Life is good.

Then the chip in my head starts to buzz...

DONOVAN
CREED
7

VEGAS
MOON

2 MILLION COPIES AND COUNTING...
JOHN LOCKE

PROLOGUE

I

JIM "LUCKY" PETERS was in Jamaica, getting a colonoscopy from a Rastafarian proctologist, when his cell phone started buzzing.

"Wha's that, Hon?" the doctor said to his nurse. "Some sarta buzzin' sound."

She located Lucky's cell phone, frowned, confiscated it. Lucky was half-conscious, and loopy enough from the "relaxing" medicine not to care. What he did care about was whatever the hell Dr. Gayle was doing in his lower tract.

"You're gonta feel some pressure, now, Mon," he said.

Pressure?

Understatement.

Was Dr. Gayle drilling for oil? Impaling him through the ass with a flagpole?

"If you're looking for Jimmy Hoffa, I can tell you right now, he's not in there," Lucky said, through clenched teeth.

"Who's Jimmy Hoffa, Mon?"

"Seriously. You push that thing any deeper, you'll scratch the back of my eyeballs!"

"Almost done, Mon, and clean as a whistle she is."

The pain and suffering was all on Lucky, since he decided to forego the anesthetic. Like all his decisions, this one had been a calculated risk.

Lucky Peters knows a lot about risk. And reward, and odds of every sort. He's a legendary gambler, allegedly worth something above fifty million dollars, the man Las Vegas casinos fear more than any other. More than they used to fear the mob, even. When Lucky sets the line on a game, casino owners hold their breath. When he wins, they shit their pants. On any given day of the week, Lucky's got a million bucks riding the line. And three times that on the weekend. And historically, sixty-eight percent of the time he wins.

Lucky's success is based on vigilance, and keeping up with the constant flux in the betting landscape. Case in point: last time he went under the knife he accepted the anesthetic, missed the injury report on Packer cornerback Johnny Sullivan, and it cost him eighty large!

So, never again.

One p.m., still in Kingston Hospital but significantly recovered, Lucky located his cell phone among his belongings and saw he had four messages, all from world-renowned plastic surgeon, Dr. Phyllis Willis. Lucky pressed the replay button to retrieve the first one.

"Lucky, this is Phyllis. Connor Payne is in the lobby of my practice! What should I do? Please call me back!" Dr. Willis sounded frantic.

Suddenly Lucky wasn't feeling so lucky. A cold chill swept through his body. Connor Payne was an international assassin. If he was in Dr. Willis's lobby, it could only mean he had information that could eventually lead to Lucky.

Second message started.

"My receptionist told Connor Payne I'm in the middle of a procedure. He doesn't believe her. He's giving me two minutes to come out, then he's coming to get me. Should I call the police? I don't know what to do! I'm terrified. Please call!"

Lucky closed his eyes. This didn't sound good.

Third message came on.

"I'm making a corporate decision. I'm in the bathroom, the door's locked. I've got the controller. I'm going to punch in the code and melt his brain right where he stands. I can't see any other way out of this. Okay, I'm hanging up. I'm going to do it. Please forgive me!"

Lucky pressed the pause button, thinking, Please don't kill him. They'll do an autopsy and find the chip we implanted in his brain. On the other hand, Dr. Phyllis Willis was a surgeon. Maybe she could slice his head open and retrieve the chip before anyone finds out what killed him.

Lucky shook his head. That was ridiculous. First of all, the receptionist, Shelby, was a witness. Second, there'd be no reason for Phyllis to slice open the brain of a man who suddenly died in the lobby of her building. If pressed by the police, Phyllis would crack and tell everything she knew. Lucky had half his life's savings invested in Ropic Industries, a company whose stock had been slipping for months. This type of news could send it into free fall.

Lucky noted the time of the calls. All four were back-to-back, made in the space of three minutes. He reminded himself that whatever he was about to hear had taken place two hours ago. It had already happened, and there was nothing he could do now, but listen how it played out. Lucky took a deep breath, hit the play button on his cell phone.

"Mr. Peters, I-I entered the code. I entered the code, b—but he's still alive! He's moving through the office! I—I think he may have killed Shelby! Oh, dear God! There are five people here. Connor Payne is going to kill us all! I can't believe you never called me back! I'm going to die today."

3

Phyllis paused a moment, then said, "I need to tell you something. Two things. First, I don't regret our affair. I'm glad we did it, because…well, because I love you. I always have and always will. And second, you need to know where I hid the device. Since the code didn't work, you'll need the device to reset it."

Phyllis paused again, as if listening for Connor Payne. Then she whispered, "Don't be angry. What I did was really stupid, but—"

On the phone, Phyllis suddenly went into full-blown panic mode. "Shit! Here he comes! I—I love you, Lucky!"

II

LUCKY NEEDED TO…not panic. He tried not panicking for awhile, but his heart was racing a mile a minute. He decided to think, instead. Okay, so he needed to make some calls.

Several calls. How many, exactly?

Three.

But who first?

Phyllis? His wife, Gwen? Mob boss Carmine Porrello?

Phyllis's cell phone went unanswered. When he called her office, a cop said, "This is Detective Scrapple. I'm logging calls for Dr. Willis. Could you state your name, please, and your relationship to Dr. Willis?"

Lucky hung up. He knew it was a stupid thing to do, since Phyllis's cell phone records would show he was the last person she called before her murder. Assuming she's dead.

Assuming?

Of course she's dead! Or she'd have called him.

Damn good thing I can prove I was in Jamaica when it happened, he thought. Of course, the details of his affair with Phyllis might come to light. Then again, beyond the cold shoulder he could expect from Gwen, a public affair could enhance his reputation as a ladies' man. A plus, in a town like Vegas.

If Lucky was anything, he was lucky. He calculated the odds of surviving Phyllis's murder relatively unscathed, and put them at 12 to 1.

Connor Payne was a different matter.

Did Phyllis tell him about Lucky's connection to the device? If so, Lucky and Gwen were both in danger.

Lucky called Gwen's cell.

No answer.

He tried their home.

No answer.

This was a problem. If Gwen's cell phone was operating, her voice message would have come on. He caught himself wishing he'd taken Gwen to Jamaica. It would've been nice to have a friendly face here, but he'd wanted to sample the local talent. He didn't get far with the Jamaican women, though. In fact, he never got started. Because by the time he landed he was already shitting blood through his shorts. After gagging everyone in first class and then baggage claim, Lucky caught a cab and went straight to the hospital. After a day of tests and prep, they scheduled his colonoscopy. Welcome to the Islands, indeed, Lucky thought.

His third call got a response.

Mob boss Carmine "The Chin" Porrello couldn't wait to take Lucky's call. He'd been trying to infiltrate Lucky's sports betting empire for years. But so far, Lucky had managed to resist the charms of doing business with the mob.

"What's up?" Carmine said.

"You know this hit man, Connor Payne?"

"Never heard of him."

"Really?"

"Really. Why you askin'?"

"He might be after me."

"Sounds like you got a problem."

"I need a bodyguard."

"If your boy's for real, none a' my people are gonna want the job."

"I just need a name. Who's the best hit man in the business?"

"By business, you mean the family?"

"No. In the world. Is there someone who's considered the best in the world?"

"Only one can be the best. But you'll never get him."

"Why?"

"He don't need the money."

Lucky said, "You give me the name, I'll get him to work for me."

"Things like this ain't free."

"You can't give me a flippin' name?"

"Not this name. Not for free."

"Fine. How much?"

"Ten."

"Ten grand? For a name?"

"Yeah, that's right. But it's a helluva name. Someone asks you for it, you can get your money back."

"Yeah, but ten g's?"

"Ten. Nothing less."

"Fuck. Okay, done. What's the name?"

Carmine's voice went low. "My part ends when I say the name. You don't tell no one I gave it to you, *capisca*?"

"Fine. What's the name?"

Carmine paused, as if looking around before saying it. "Donovan Creed," he whispered.

"What's his number?"

"What? You think I know his fuckin' number?"

"What'd I just pay you ten large for, if not his number?"

PREVIEW

"His name, asshole."

"How am I going to find his number?" Lucky said.

"That'll cost you."

"How much?"

"Five more."

"You gotta be shitting me."

"Let me tell you somethin', Lucky."

"Yeah?"

"When someone wants this man's name and number, they're humpin' their last chicken."

Lucky paused. "I don't have any idea what you just said."

"Ah, shit. I'm gettin' old. There's an expression in there somewhere. I just can't remember the fuckin' thing. You want the number, or what?"

"Yeah, fine."

Carmine gave a number.

"What's this, his cell phone?"

"No. Sal Bonadello's."

"Who the fuck is that?" Lucky said.

"The guy that can get you Creed."

III

IT COSTS LUCKY another ten grand to finally get Donovan Creed on the phone. When he does, it goes like this:

"Mr. Creed, this is Jim Peters, from Las Vegas. My friends call me Lucky."

Dead silence.

"Are you there?"

"Sorry, I thought you were making a speech."

"Where are you, Mr. Creed? I mean, are you in the States?"

"Mr. Peters, I'll be glad to tell you where I am, but it'll cost you an ear."

"A...what? Did you say an ear? What are you talking about?"

"You want something personal from me, I get something of yours in return. Since you asked, I'm in—"

"Shit no!" Lucky screams. "Don't tell me!"

The voice on the other end is calm. "Fair enough. Why are we speaking today?"

"Ever hear of a guy named Connor Payne?"

"I have."

"What do you know about him?"

"He's one of the most lethal people in the world. Why do you ask?"

"I have reason to believe he murdered a friend of mine a few hours ago."

"A close friend?"

"Well...yes. I mean, she was the Medical Director of a corporation I invested in. I'm the majority stockholder."

"Wow. So Connor Payne murdered your friend."

"Yes."

"What are you going to do about it?"

"Me? I...well...I mean, I'm trying to do something about it right now. By calling you."

"Did you have sex with her just the two times, or has this been going on awhile?"

"I—what? No. I mean, we did business together. We had a professional relationship."

"Are you telling me Phyllis Willis was a hooker?"

"What? No, of course not. I mean, wait—how did you know her name?"

"It's my job to know. By the way, were you able to keep your polyp?"

"My...polyp? What polyp?"

"The one Dr. Gayle cut out of your colon this morning."

"He...I mean...what?"

Creed made a tsk, tsk sound. "Let me guess: he told you there was nothing in there."

"His exact words were, I was clean as a whistle."

"He keeps them, you know."

"Polyps?"

"Yup."

"Why?"

"Makes necklaces out of them. Sells them on the Broomilaw."

"The Broomilaw?"

10

"When it ices over. Between bear fights."

This conversation has completely gotten away from Lucky. He starts over. "Mr. Creed, I want to hire you."

"You want me to get your polyp back?"

"I want you to protect me from Connor Payne."

"Whew."

"Excuse me?"

"Thank God you're asking for something simple."

"Simple?"

"Compared to getting your polyp back."

Lucky was getting frustrated. "Are you sure you're Donovan Creed?"

"Pretty sure."

"The Donovan Creed who kills people?"

"Are you recording this conversation?"

"Of course not!"

"Too bad. I've been working on my tough-guy voice. I was hoping to hear how it comes across over the phone."

"Mr. Creed."

"Yes?"

"I'm a wealthy man. I can pay you to protect me. How much would you charge?"

"Depends on what you want. Do I just have to keep you alive, or would I have to kill Connor Payne?"

"You...could kill him?"

"I could. But I doubt I'll have to."

"Why not?"

"If he knows I'm guarding you, he won't come within ten miles of us."

"If that's true, I shouldn't have to pay you very much," Lucky said.

"That's a rather odd way to look at it."

11

"I'll pay you twenty grand a week. How does that sound?"

"Paltry."

"Are you kidding me?"

"A premium hooker would cost you thirty. And offer no protection against Connor Payne."

"I don't need a hooker."

"You might, if you're right about Phyllis being dead."

Lucky sighed. "Look. You want the job or not?"

"Mr. Peters?"

"Yeah?"

"You're a liar, a cheat, and a cheapskate."

"Based on?"

"You lied about fucking Phyllis. You cheated on your wife. And you don't want to pay me a fair price to save your life."

Lucky paused. When he spoke, he sounded dejected. "How'd you know about Phyllis?"

"Carmine told me."

"Carmine Porrello?"

"You know any other Carmines?"

"He said he didn't know you! That sonofabitch charged me fifteen grand for Sal's phone number! And Sal charged me ten for yours!"

"So you'll pay twenty-five grand to get me on the phone, but only twenty a week to protect you? That hurts, Mr. Peters. If I have to seek therapy over this, who's going to stop Connor Payne from killing you?"

"I can kill him myself."

"Now that's a bold statement."

"There's a device. I only need you as long as it takes to find it."

"Interesting. Tell me more."

"I can't. Not over the phone. If you protect Gwen till I get back to Vegas, you and I can search Phyllis's office together, and find this thing I'm looking for."

"Gwen?"

"My wife. Her life could be in danger."

"Why?"

"If Connor Payne thinks I have the device, he might go to my house looking for it."

"Or for you."

"Right."

"But you don't have it."

"No. Phyllis has…had it."

"Want me to check her office?"

"You can't. The police are there. You can get me in there tonight, though, right?"

"If I come to Vegas," Creed said.

Lucky said, "How did Carmine know about Phyllis?"

"Mr. Peters, you may be brilliant when it comes to bookmaking, but you don't know shit about the people who are scheming to bring you down."

"And you do?"

"What I don't know I can figure out."

"But you won't help me."

"Did I say that?"

"You said I was a liar, a cheat, and a cheapskate."

"True. Nevertheless, I'm in."

"You are?"

"I'm intrigued."

"Why?"

"Connor Payne is a one-man army. I want to know how you plan to kill him."

PREVIEW

"I'll tell you tonight, after I land. There's a direct flight to Vegas, leaves at five, gets there nine twenty. I need you to go to my house, watch my wife till then."

"Okay."

"And bring her with you to the airport to meet my plane."

"You need to let her know I'm coming."

"Of course."

"There's one problem."

"What?"

"The police are having a convention at your house."

"How do you know?"

"Carmine told me."

Lucky's heart sinks. "You don't think something's happened to Gwen, do you?"

"No."

"You sure?"

"Positive."

"Why?"

"No ambulance."

"Mr. Creed. Are you in fact in Las Vegas?"

"Let's put it like this: I can be at your house in an hour."

"And you'll take the job?"

"If you agree to cooperate."

"What would I have to do?"

"Tell me everything."

"Everything?"

"That's right."

"About Connor Payne?"

"We can start with him and see where it takes us."

"Fine. But I can't divulge any details about my business."

"Why not?"

"It could ruin me."

"Let me put it this way. You can tell me what I want to know, or you can tell Connor Payne everything. And he won't ask nicely."

1.

29 Hours Earlier...

THE CHIP IN my head can be activated by tapping a four-digit code into a device that looks like a wristwatch. When the code is entered, the chip heats up and starts liquefying my brain. Do that to me, and you better have fresh batteries and type in the right code, because if you don't, I'm going to come for you.

It's not personal.

I know you've got a life, a loving spouse, two apple-cheeked kids, three dogs, four cats and five parakeets. Or maybe you live alone in a basement apartment with a single window that's half dirt and half sky, and you dine nightly on canned cat food while fantasizing about large, hairy women in boxer shorts who could win the limbo contest if the people on either end would just raise the fucking bar!

Either way, you've got a life, and as far as I'm concerned, you deserve to live it without interference from me.

Until you press those buttons.

Do that, and your life belongs to me.

I'm Donovan Creed, former CIA assassin, sometime hit man for the mob. I currently head up a team of assassins who kill suspected terrorists for Uncle Sam. I can be your best friend or your worst nightmare.

But you should know I don't have many friends.

I'm a tolerant, even-tempered guy who likes the same things you do: long walks on the beach at sunset, holding hands, romantic candle-lit dinners featuring great food and premium Kentucky bourbon, making love under the stars with high-end call girls, torturing, maiming and killing bad guys...

I'm not a bully.

Random comment, I know, but God, I hate bullies.

I've been told I have a hero complex, which means I feel compelled to help those in need. Personally, I think the world would be a better place if more people get involved when bad things go down. But apparently the fact I feel compelled to help people—instead of choosing to help them, makes me something of a sociopath. Let's say it this way: if you're a bully—and that word covers a lot of ground with me—it won't take long for you to see something no one wants to see:

The man I keep hid.

To prevent that from happening, don't fuck with the USA, and don't fuck with me, or the people I care about.

Which brings me to the buzz I felt in my head a few hours ago. The one caused not by alcohol, but by someone attempting to activate the kill chip in my brain.

I'd been enjoying a lovely dinner with Miranda, a particularly attractive young lady of the evening. We were in New York City, had the whole night ahead of us. I didn't cancel the date, because we'd been looking forward to it for weeks. In the end, we had a great time despite the fact someone was trying to kill me.

Here's what I know about the kill chip: it was grafted to my brain more than a year ago by the government surgeon who heads the hospital at Sensory Resources, a secret facility in northwest Virginia, where I have an office and a jail cell I sleep in from time to time. By choice. Doc Howard implanted the chip while I was in a coma, under his care. Unfortunately, it can't be removed without rendering me brain-dead. When I found out what he'd done, guess what I did about it?

Nothing.

Crazy, right? But as it turned out, Doc had been following orders from my boss, Darwin, who wanted the means to snuff me at will. By telling me about the chip, Doc Howard did me a favor, though he charged me a hundred million dollars. He gave me a controller, the code, and showed me how to change it. As a plus, he explained that if Darwin ever tried to kill me, I'd feel a buzzing in my head.

But the buzzing I felt at dinner had nothing to do with Darwin. I know, because the device requires GPS, and Darwin was in an underground bunker all night, hosting a Homeland Security meeting.

Miranda gives me a long, sensual kiss and asks me to stay. I know it's part of the service, and she doesn't mean it, but it's nice to hear, anyway. I mean, she obviously likes me more than she has to, but I maintain no illusions about our relationship. It's tit for cash. Still, had the attempt on my life not been made, I would've stayed.

I love falling asleep in a woman's arms.

Reluctantly, I leave Miranda's house and walk to my limo. After getting comfortable, I call Doc Howard, who predictably complains about the time of night. I tell him about the buzzing in my head earlier, and he says he'll look into it.

I say, "Look into it now, because I'm coming to see you."

I get Lou Kelly, my facilitator, to book me a jet helicopter. He does, but it won't be ready for two hours. My limo driver takes me back to the hotel to pack my bags and check out.

18

Then we wait an hour by the private airstrip till the chopper shows up.

An hour after that I land on the Sensory Resources helipad. I have enough time to take a shower and drink a protein shake before meeting with Doc Howard. When he finally arrives, I start right in on him. "Two weeks ago I wired a hundred million to your offshore account in return for a bypass code."

"Yes." Doc Howard is visibly nervous, as he should be. Who can blame him? I'm not happy.

"You told me no one else had access to the code," I say, knowing that's not entirely true.

"I said to the best of my knowledge no one had it, but if someone did, and tried to access it, you'd feel buzzing in your head."

"Only problem is, I don't know who pressed the button last night."

"I've been thinking about that," Doc said.

"And?"

"There was someone present when I implanted the chip."

"What? Who?"

"The medical director of the company that manufactured it."

"And you decided not to tell me this because?"

"I was afraid you'd kill her, to tie up the loose end."

"I didn't kill you."

"No, but at the time, I didn't know you could be reasoned with."

"I try to give people a chance, Doc."

"You would have killed her."

"Probably. In the end. I mean, I'm walking around with a bomb in my head and she's got the code that can set it off.

She's a major threat."

"I didn't consider her a threat at the time."

"Because?"

"I thought she had no way to access the code, once we changed it."

"But that wasn't true, was it?"

"Apparently not. I think the company lied about the device."

"You're quite astute. I hadn't realized till now."

"I note your sarcasm," Doc Howard says. "But yes. There has to be a master device that can reset the code."

I shake my head.

"I'm sorry," he says.

"That's comforting."

Doc Howard is short, pudgy, middle-aged, with thick glasses and a kindly grandfather's face. He's looking at me with less fear than he'd shown earlier. He knows he's valuable to me for reasons that would take too long to list.

But I'll give you one: he does all our body-double surgeries. I've got people all over the country guarding other people who don't even know they're being guarded. They're body doubles for my hit squad, my family, my closest friends. I need Doc Howard, and we've always gotten along. I don't resent him charging me for sharing his secret. Proves he trusts me more than he trusts Darwin.

On the other hand, who wouldn't?

"I want names and addresses," I say.

"Her name is Phyllis Willis."

I look at him. "Don't make me lose my patience."

"Swear to God, that's her name: Dr. Phyllis Willis."

"And she works where?"

"Ropic Industries, Las Vegas."

"What do they do?"

"I don't know. Darwin set it up. I only know about the chip."

"Is Dr. Willis in-house?"

"No. She's a plastic surgeon."

"In Vegas?"

"I think so. But wherever she is, I'm sure Lou Kelly's guys can find her."

"We didn't have this conversation, Doc."

"Of course not."

I pause. "You should've told me."

"I was trying to save a life. I'm sorry."

I turn to leave. Doc Howard says, "Phyllis thinks your name is Connor Payne."

"What?"

"That's the name—"

I hold up my hand. "I remember. That's good. I can use it to my advantage."

He nods, relieved.

DONOVAN
CREED

DONOVAN CREED works as an assassin for an elite branch of Homeland Security. When he isn't killing terrorists, he moonlights as a hit man for the mob, and tests torture weapons for the Army. Donovan Creed is a very tough guy.

To discover more – and some tempting special offers – why not visit our website: www.headofzeus.com

MEET THE AUTHOR

John Locke is the first writer to sell over a million self-published ebooks on Amazon. Every ebook he has written and published has been a bestseller. Visit www.donovancreed.com